She breathed [barcode: D0541388] **and felt the sn against her f his muscles under her fingers.**

This man deserved so much more than this.

He deserved love and happiness, and a daughter who idolised him. Not this battered mess of a life. Luke let out one more heart-wrenching sigh, and then she felt his muscles slacken. She was pretty sure he was over the worst now, but she'd better stay put for another few minutes, just to make sure.

How arrogant she'd been to think she could fix this family. In truth, she didn't know where to start. She was way out of her depth. One thing she could do was make sure he got a good night's sleep. She'd bet he didn't get too many of those.

So she lay snuggled against him, and cried for the wasted years and the horrors he must have endured. And when she had finished she placed one tender kiss on his back and closed her eyes.

First published in Great Britain 2007
Harlequin Mills & Boon Limited,
Eton House, 18-24 Paradise Road, Richmond, Surrey TW9 1SR

© Fiona Harper 2007

ISBN-13: 978 0 263 85419 0
ISBN-10:   0 263 85419 1

Set in Times Roman 11¾ on 13½ pt
02-0307-58568

Printed and bound in Spain
by Litografia Rosés, S.A., Barcelona

As a child, **Fiona Harper** was constantly teased for either having her nose in a book, or living in a dream world. Things haven't changed much since then, but at least in writing she's found a use for her runaway imagination. After studying dance at university, Fiona worked as a dancer, teacher and choreographer, before trading in that career for video-editing and production. When she became a mother she cut back on her working hours to spend time with her children, and when her littlest one started pre-school she found a few spare moments to rediscover an old but not forgotten love—writing.

Fiona lives in London, but her other favourite places to be are the Highlands of Scotland and the Kent countryside on a summer's afternoon. She loves cooking, good food and anything cinnamon-flavoured. Of course she still can't keep away from a good book, or a good movie—especially romances—but only if she's stocked up with tissues, because she knows she will need them by the end, be it happy or sad. Her favourite things in the world are her wonderful husband, who has learned to decipher her incoherent ramblings, and her two daughters.

Recent titles by the same author:

BLIND-DATE MARRIAGE*

*Fiona's first book for Mills & Boon® Romance
won the distinguished
Romantic Novelists' Association Joan Hessayon
New Writers' Award 2006

For Andy, my own grumpy hero.

CHAPTER ONE

STUPID map!

Gaby stood on the deserted quay and cursed herself for being on the wrong side of the river. She reached through the open car door for the map book and squinted at it. Then she turned it sideways and squinted again.

David had always said she was useless at map-reading. Mind you, her ex-husband had said she was useless at most things. She'd spent the last year doing her utmost to prove him wrong and it rankled that one of his thousand-and-one reasons to leave her had some foundation.

She slammed the car door and looked back across the river.

Lower Hadwell was only a quarter of a mile away as the crow flies, but it would take her at least an hour to drive to the nearest town with a bridge and navigate her way back to the little village.

Botheration! Her first prospect of a proper job in almost a decade and she was already late for the interview. And not just fashionably late. She was all out, start-calling-the-hospitals late.

David's mocking face filled her mind. 'Shut up!' she said out loud. Stupid, but it made her feel better.

She looked down at the map and a slow smile crept across her face. A little line of blue dashes. There was a ferry! Not so useless after all. Hah!

On one side of the quay a steep ramp led down to a shingle beach exposed by the receding tide. How on earth was she going to get the car down there without it rolling into the river? She blessed her sensible driving shoes and walked halfway down the ramp to get a better look.

'Afternoon.'

The gravelly voice that came out of nowhere almost had her speeding back to London on foot. She put a hand over her stampeding heart and faced the stocky man who'd stood up from inspecting a rather unseaworthy-looking boat. He was so much a part of the scenery she hadn't noticed him before. She half expected him to be covered with the same vivid green weed and barnacles as the ailing boat.

'Oh, good afternoon.' She smiled. 'I was wondering about the ferry. Do you know what the timetable is?'

'This time of year it don't have one.'

'Oh.'

He went back to examining a broken bit of wood and she waited for him to continue, hands clasped in front of her. When it became apparent that he believed their conversation to be over, she crunched her way across the shingle towards him and stopped a few feet away.

He looked up at her again, his face crinkled against the February sun. She had no idea how old he was. The tattooed skin of his arms was smooth, but his face was etched like an old man's. He looked as if he'd spent most of his life scrunching his face against the reflection of the sun on the water, and the salt and wind had weathered it into deep furrows.

He didn't speak, but nodded in the direction of a large post in the car park. A brass bell crusted with verdigris hung from it. There was a sign, but she couldn't read it from down here on the beach, so back up the ramp she went.

Underneath the brief timetable was the following information: '30th October to 30th March—Please ring bell to call the ferryman.'

Great! South Devon was obviously still operating on medieval principles.

She took hold of the frayed rope that hung from it and flung the clapper hard against the brass. The salty-looking boatman looked up, wiped his hands on the back of his jeans and sauntered up the slope.

'Yes?' he said, folding his face up even further.

Gaby shook her head and looked at him hard. Perhaps all those stories about in-breeding in rural communities were true. She spoke slowly, pronouncing each word carefully. 'I want to take my car across on the ferry.'

He threw his head back and laughed and suddenly she had the horrible feeling the tables had been turned and she was the one with the single-digit IQ. She brushed the thought away and stood a little taller.

'There's a ramp, isn't there?'

He rubbed a stubby hand across his mouth and brought the rumbles of laughter to a halt. 'Yep. And that over there is the ferryboat.'

She turned to where he pointed. A small boat, maybe fifteen feet in length, with a square cabin at the front and wooden benches round the back was tied to a ring near a mossy flight of steps.

The map book was still in her hand and she pulled it back in front of her face.

Passenger ferry, it said. Okay, so it wasn't just map-reading she had a problem with, but reading in general.

She lowered the book to find him still looking at her. He obviously thought she was unspeakably dim, but he was grinning. Probably glad of the entertainment.

'Hop in,' he said. 'Your car'll be fine here. Last ferry back has to be before six, mind. I go off duty then.'

Her lips pressed together while she thought of something to say. Phrases whirled round her head and the moment slid away until anything she said would just sound forced. So, in the end, she just smiled back, locked her car and followed him down the steps to the ferry.

When he turned to start the motor she scrubbed her face with her hands and half-sighed, half-chuckled. You had to be able to laugh at yourself, right? One thing she'd learnt since her divorce was not to be so worried about doing or saying the wrong thing. Nobody was perfect, after all. Now, if only she could remember that on the next visit to her parents. Especially when they sighed and exchanged glances.

She knew what they thought. She must have been a terrible wife if she couldn't keep a 'catch' like David happy. Her husband had traded her in for a newer, more compact model and it *must* be her fault. Nothing to do with the fact he was a self-centred, tyrannical little…

She turned her face into the wind so it blew her long brown hair behind her and stuffed her hands into the pockets of her fleece.

Lower Hadwell sat hibernating on the far side of the river, the ice-cream colours of the cottages muted by the winter sun. A narrow road separated a row of houses from the beach, then curved up a steep hill lined by cottages and shops, tightly packed as if huddling together for warmth.

Strange, that a picture-postcard village like this could contain a man with such a dark past. She wondered if they knew. Did the locals close ranks and whisper when he walked into the pub, or had they welcomed him into their little community? She hoped it was the latter. He deserved a fresh start, far away from the twitching net curtains of the suburbs.

Soon the ferry came alongside the string of pontoons that trailed down the beach from the village. The tide was so low that only the last two or three were floating. The rest lay helpless on the shingle, waiting for the murky water to rise and give them some purpose.

Gaby paid the ferryman and hopped out of the boat. No one was around. Well, almost no one. A lone figure in an oversized red fleece stood at the edge of one pontoon, hunched over and staring into the water. It was a girl, not more than eleven or twelve years old, her long dark hair scraped into a severe ponytail. Now and then she looked up and just stared into the distance.

Gaby knew that look. She'd spent many hours as child staring out of her bedroom window wearing the same heavy expression. Wishing her life were different, wishing she'd been born in a different time or a different place.

The girl looked up when she heard Gaby approaching but turned away instantly, more out of sheer disinterest than embarrassment. After a minute or so she lifted a string out of the water to reveal a hook, a small circular weight and some long, stringy bait. She stared at the lonely hook and her shoulders drooped even further.

Gaby itched to say something, to let the girl know the feeling wouldn't last for ever. One day she'd be free. In the end she said, 'Never mind. Maybe you'll catch a fish next time.'

A small huff was her only answer.

'What's that stuff on the hook, anyway?'

The girl dropped the line back into the water with a plop and wearily turned to face her. 'My dad told me not to talk to strangers.'

'Very sensible advice.'

Advice she should follow herself. The girl turned away and focused her attention on the fishing line once again.

Gaby frowned and wondered whether she was transposing her own childhood worries on to this lone figure. Perhaps she should just leave the girl alone to catch whatever it was she was trying to catch, even though her intuition told her that what the girl really wanted was not going to be found at the end of some orange twine.

Come on, Gaby! You've already given yourself a stern talking to about getting too embroiled in other people's business. You don't have time to comfort sad little girls on the jetty, no matter how big their eyes or how lonely they look. You've got a job to grovel for.

She'd only taken a couple of steps when the girl spoke.

'It's bacon.'

Gaby stopped and walked back a few steps. 'What kind of fish like bacon? Don't tell me there are sharks in there.'

The girl almost smiled. She started hauling the string out of the grey-green water again. 'Not fish! Look.'

On the end of the line were three small crabs, the largest the size of the girl's hand. They were beautiful colours—shades of rust, green and slate. All three were hanging on to the string for dear life and fighting for the turgid bait. The girl shook the line over a water-filled bucket and two plopped into it to join a seething mass of crabs, all struggling to work out where that darn bit of bacon had gone.

The girl gave the line a more vigorous shake to dislodge the stubborn one still clinging on in hope of a square meal. This was a crafty little sucker, though. When the line shook a second time it catapulted itself beyond the rim of the bucket and scuttled towards Gaby's feet. She shrieked and ran down the pontoon.

The girl burst out laughing.

Meanwhile, the kamikaze crab ignored the commotion and lobbed itself off the edge of the pontoon and sank without a trace. Gaby edged back towards the girl and her bucket. It was good to see her smiling, but she reminded herself she needed to get on. Perhaps the girl could help her find him. She pulled a scrap of paper from her pocket and read the hastily scribbled address.

'Do you know where the Old Boathouse is, by any chance?' she asked, keeping as far away from the bucket as possible.

The smile faded from the girl's face. She gave Gaby a long hard look and tipped her head to one side. 'Why do you want to go there?'

'Um…it's business.' That was vague enough to cover all eventualities. The girl looked unconvinced. Still, she pointed to a stone building that seemed to be sitting on the curving shore about a quarter of a mile away.

'How do I get there? Is there a boat?'

The girl shook her head. 'There's a lane opposite the Ferryboat Inn.' She stopped and looked at Gaby's suede trainers. 'It's a bit muddy, though.'

She thanked the girl and walked up a ramp and on to the main street. The opening to the lane wasn't hard to find. Before her view was blocked by a line of trees, she looked back towards the river.

The girl picked up her bucket, tipped the angry contents into the river and started all over again.

Muddy? It was practically a swamp!

Gaby lifted her foot and tried to work out whether she could actually still see her trainers through the mud boots she seemed to be wearing. The cold was seeping though the suede and into the bones of her feet.

She was hardly going to look the picture of professionalism when she reached her destination. Her thoughts strayed to the nice jacket and sensible-but-smart shoes still in her car. It might have been a good idea to spruce herself up before she'd got on the ferry, but she'd figured that, since she was almost two hours late, the absence of correct footwear and her one good jacket were the least of her worries.

Soon she caught glimpses of the Old Boathouse through the leafless trees. It was a large building made of local stone. Even to her untrained eye it was obvious that it had once been what its name suggested. Over the years—she wouldn't like to guess how many—it had been extended, and the half of the house that faced the lane had the appearance of a quaint country cottage with leaded windows and a dry stone wall enclosing the garden.

She was just nearing the sturdy gate when a man appeared from behind the house. She stopped in her tracks. Who was that? The gardener? He looked dishevelled enough, but something about the clothes was wrong.

An image from a TV news bulletin flashed across her mind.

That was him? The man she'd come to see?

Her feet sank further into the mud and she listened to the sound of her own breath. He didn't even notice her. He just loaded a large cardboard box into the back of a Range Rover and disappeared back inside the house.

He looked different. Leaner. Harder.

His sandy hair was longer and messier and he obviously hadn't been near a razor in a couple of days. Gone was the respectable-looking doctor, replaced by a wilder, more rugged-looking man. Oh, yes, five years in prison had definitely changed Luke Armstrong.

Suddenly he reappeared. And this time he saw her.

At first his face registered surprise, but it quickly

hardened into something else. He dumped the box he was carrying in the boot of the car and strode towards her.

'What do you want?'

He barked the question out and her heart started to gallop inside her chest. She'd never been very good at confrontation and he seemed ready for a fight. As she struggled to make her lips form her own name, he looked her up and down. And if looks were anything to go by, she knew she'd been fired even before the interview.

'Mr Armstrong?' she stammered.

'You know full well who I am.'

Well, of course she did! She was hoping to be his new nanny.

'I'm sure you know what brand of toothpaste I use, so don't turn up here looking all innocent and pretend you've lost your way. I've heard that one before.'

She certainly *didn't* know what toothpaste he used! What was he trying to imply? A sudden rush of heat behind her eyes told her she was more ready for confrontation than she'd suspected. 'Mr Armstrong, I assure you—'

'I wouldn't believe a word that came out of your lying mouth.' The fury in his eyes stopped any retort she might have had to hand. His face twisted as he shook his head, then he just turned and walked back towards the house. Gaby was so shocked that it didn't even occur to her to move.

Just before he disappeared from view, he turned to look over his shoulder. 'You'll just have to tell your editor you blew it,' he yelled. And then he was gone.

Editor? He'd said editor, she was sure of it.

Oh…

Now she got it. He thought she was a journalist. She looked down and tried to see what it was about her appearance that had set him down that path. Slightly ageing fleece, go-with-anything black trousers and a pair of comfy driving shoes under a layer of mud. Didn't look much like a journalist to her. But then, she didn't look much like a top-notch nanny either.

She let out a long breath and her anger turned tide. No wonder he'd reacted the way he had. The tabloids had given him a really rough ride before, during and after his trial. She'd followed the story in the papers and it hadn't been pretty.

Luke Armstrong had been charged with his wife's murder after she'd been found dead in a hotel room in Kent. Each gory detail had been received more thirstily than the last.

'DOCTOR KILLS WIFE IN CRIME OF PASSION!' the headline had screamed.

The prosecution had argued that he'd followed her, leaving his young daughter in the care of a neighbour, and found his wife enjoying the luxuries of a country house hotel with another man. In a fit of rage he'd struck out. Mrs Armstrong had fallen and hit her head. And, while she lay bleeding all over the Chinese rug, he'd fled and hadn't returned home for hours.

Of course, he'd denied it. And he'd been so convincing in court the jury would probably have acquitted him if it hadn't been for the forensic evidence. When he'd stood in the witness stand, he'd sworn he'd only got as far as the hotel lobby, where he'd seen his wife and her lover lace fingers and climb the stairs together. He said he'd driven off on to the North Downs and sat in his car, trying to work out what to do next.

But DNA evidence had made his words into a fairy tale. He'd been in the hotel room the night his wife had died.

Then, five years later, when the public had forgotten all about the doctor in his prison cell, there had been another headline:

'DOCTOR CLEARED OF WIFE'S MURDER!'

She remembered something about cross-contamination of samples at the lab.

Of course, now the nation was truly sorry. Never had believed it anyway. He'd always looked like such a nice man…

But he didn't look so nice any more, thought Gaby, as she remembered the way he'd towered over her only seconds before.

It was strange. After reading all the newspaper reports, even though they'd never been introduced, had never chatted, she felt as if she knew this man.

Not the stupid details, like his favourite colour or
how he liked his coffee. But she knew he was honest
and caring and fiercely loyal to those he loved. She
knew the things that mattered.

And it was for this reason, and this reason alone,
she was going to make him listen to her, rather than
walk back down the lane and head home.

CHAPTER TWO

WELL, if she was going to face him, she couldn't just stand here getting muddier by the second. But, as much as she wanted to help, she didn't relish facing the snarling man who'd just stomped into the house, either. It was that look in his eyes, the look that said she was worthless, stupid and way out of her league.

Of course, the look really wasn't for her. It was for the phantom journalist he'd taken her for. But she'd seen the same look in David's eyes many a time, and it made something inside her wither. When her ex-husband had looked at her like that, he'd known exactly who he was talking to.

Gaby smoothed her hair back with her hands and walked up to the front door. Her heart pounded in time with the three sharp raps she gave with the knocker. She waited, ears straining for a sound, but there was nothing. Just as she was about to knock again, she heard a door slam somewhere inside, and she thought better of it.

He knew she was out here; he was just ignoring her.

She sighed and rubbed her face with her hands. She'd driven for over seven hours to get here. She was cold and her feet were soggy, and she wasn't going to just turn round and go home again because Luke Armstrong was in a strop.

She followed his footprints round to the back of the house, where she found the back door slightly ajar. He'd probably been too fired up to make sure it had clicked shut behind him.

It gave a creak as she nudged it with her fingertips. 'Mr Armstrong?'

She peered inside and found a small room, with an even smaller window, full of sturdy boots and sensible-looking coats on hooks.

'Mr—' She swallowed the rest of her sentence as the door leading into the rest of the house crashed open.

'You people never give up, do you?'

Gaby gulped and fumbled to get her bag off her shoulder. In this tiny space he seemed much more menacing, like a caged animal.

'Get out before I call the police!'

He took a step towards her and she backed away, glancing down at the bag as she rummaged inside it. When she looked up at him again, his jaw was set like steel. Now would be a really good time to do exactly as he'd suggested and run out through the door and down the lane without looking back.

She held her breath as the air fizzled with his barely harnessed anger. And then her fingers felt the corner of the business card she'd been searching for and she pulled it out of her bag, surprised by the deftness of her own movements.

He looked slightly taken aback and she used the split-second opportunity to wave the card within his line of vision. 'Bright Sparks Agency, Mr Armstrong.'

He stared at the card, then stared at her, then stared at the card some more.

'I'm here for the interview.'

He looked at her once again, clearly astonished.

'For the nanny's position,' she offered.

The penny finally dropped. She saw a small change in his features as he marshalled his thoughts. He was still giving her a hard stare, but it lacked the zinging fury of the last one. This one felt like a defensive position rather than an attack.

'You're late.'

'I know, I'm sorry. I got a bit—'

'You'd better come inside, then.' He turned and went through the small door leading into the house and disappeared down a corridor. Gaby was about to follow him when she remembered the state of her shoes. Now her future employer—fingers crossed— had calmed to simmering point, she didn't want to do anything to raise his temperature again.

She sat down on a low bench and tried to work out how to take her shoes off while keeping her hands mud-free. Eventually she succeeded and placed them side by side under the bench. Then she hung her fleece on a hook.

Come on, Gaby! Nothing to be frightened of. He should be apologising to you, really. But she stood motionless, her feet feeling the cold of the tiled floor. Somehow, the prospect of being interviewed in her socks made her feel at a disadvantage.

Luke's face reappeared through the open door and she flinched.

'It's this way.'

He pointed down a small corridor. The only thing she could do was scurry through the house after him until they reached the kitchen.

'Coffee?'

He didn't wait for her answer, but turned to fill the kettle.

How bizarre! It was as if the whole scene outside had never happened. She'd bet there was only a slim chance of getting an apology too. But that was okay. It was so long since she'd heard anything like that pass a man's lips, she was starting to think they were genetically incapable. At least she knew what she was getting if he acted like that. Seven years of marriage to David had given her plenty of practice.

She leaned over the kitchen counter slightly to look out of the window. The river was as smooth as glass. Off in the distance she could see the jetty in the village, but no smudge of red fleece was visible.

Slowly, she became aware that he was watching her. She turned and straightened, feeling instantly as if she'd been summoned to stand in front of the head-master. He didn't smile, but he didn't look fierce either. He just seemed to be taking her in. Assessing her.

'They said they'd try to send someone, but I thought our luck had run out.'

'Pardon?'

He frowned. 'The agency. Mrs Pullman said she'd try a long shot, but she wasn't hopeful. When you were late, I assumed the long shot hadn't paid off.'

'Well, here I am—at last.' Far too bright and chirpy. She was overcompensating. 'Don't worry about…earlier. I totally understand.'

Old habits died hard. She was apologising for being in the right, yet again.

'So, as you know, I'm Luke Armstrong. Mrs Pullman didn't get around to telling me your name.'

'Gabrielle—well, Gaby, really. Michaels. Gaby Michaels.'

'Like the angels.'

'The what?'

'The archangels—in the Bible. Gabriel and Michael.'

She creased her forehead and looked at him hard. Was he making fun of her? His face was blank. In fact, he looked as if he'd forgotten how to laugh. Definitely not a joke, then.

'I'd never thought of my name that way.'

He nodded.

Boy, this guy was cryptic! She had no more idea of what he was thinking than she had of when high tide was. They were never going to get through the interview if they carried on like this.

She took a deep breath. 'How old is your daughter, then?'

'I thought I was supposed to be interviewing *you*.'

She shrugged. 'Interview away. But there are a few things I need to know before I decide if I'm…what you need.' She had been going to say *staying,* but something had stopped her. Maybe it was the fact that she suspected he hadn't always been like this, that he needed a second chance. Heaven knew she was an expert at that. Her ex had used up second, third and three-hundredth chances.

He plonked a mug of coffee in front of her and she saw his eyes glaze slightly as he slipped into autopilot. This definitely wasn't the first time he'd done this. He asked her the usual stuff at first, but then he put down his mug and looked at her.

'If you don't mind my saying, you're not what I expected. Most of the nannies I've seen have been younger and—er—dressed a little differently.'

She didn't think for a minute it would matter if she did mind, and decided she might as well be equally straightforward.

'Well, Mr Armstrong, just because I don't look like Mary Poppins, it doesn't mean I'm not competent at my job. Some children find meeting new people a little unsettling, especially if they look all starched and pressed. I find it helps if I'm more casually dressed.'

It was one of her strong points—the fact she could still remember that situations adults took for granted could be very uncomfortable for a child. It was why the agency had liked to send her off to deal with some of the 'problem' cases when she'd been working full time as a nanny. And why Mrs Pullman had phoned her up out of the blue when every available nanny on her books had baulked at taking this job. She'd jumped at the chance. It had to beat her temporary job at the riotous soft-play centre in Croydon.

'As for my age, well, I'm returning to work after a few years' break.'

'Oh?' He looked suspicious.

'When I got married, my husband preferred I didn't work.'

'And he doesn't mind now?'

'It's none of his business. We've been divorced for nearly a year.' She didn't add that her husband had got the seven year itch and had scratched it enthusiastically.

'And now you're back on the market? Job-wise, I mean,' he added hastily.

'I am.' She gave a little smile, a real one. 'Actually, I'm really looking forward to being a nanny again.'

'Well, I'm glad you decided to come out of retirement for us. Heather definitely needs an experienced hand. How soon can you start? We could do with you right now.'

She'd been planning to visit one of her old school-friends who lived in Exeter after the interview. She hadn't seen Caroline for years and was looking forward to a week of coffee and gossiping.

'Oh. I'm not sure I... Don't you want some time to think? To check references?'

His mouth pulled down at the corners and he shook his head. 'If you're good enough for the Bright Sparks Agency, you're good enough for me. And besides, I'm desperate.'

Her chair scraped on the slate floor as she stood, but before she'd even managed to say she needed time to think, the back door slammed open. She was facing the opposite direction but, from the grim look on Luke Armstrong's face, she had no doubt that his experienced-hand-needing daughter had just made her entrance.

'Heather, this is—'

A red fleece swept past the kitchen table and out into the living room. Moments later heavy feet pounded the stairs in a distant part of the house.

Luke shot to his feet, his eyes blazing.

'I'm sorry about that. She's having a difficult time adjusting at the moment. I—I'll explain later.'

With that, he forged out of the room. More heavy footsteps. Must be genetic. She couldn't have made that much noise if she were wearing lead boots. Muffled shouting. A door slammed. Then footsteps in tandem.

Luke nudged Heather into the room. Her eyes were on the floor and her bottom lip stuck out like a toddler's. 'Luke says I've got to say hello.'

'Heather!' The rising volume of his voice had Gaby shaking, but it seemed to flow off the girl. Her chin jutted more decidedly into her chest.

'Heather, I would like you to say hello to Gaby. She's going to be looking after you when I start work.'

Gaby spluttered. 'Actually, I—'

At the sound of Gaby's voice, Heather lifted her head just enough to peer out from under her fringe. 'Oh, it's you. The crab lady.'

Luke looked between the pair in astonishment.

Gaby waggled a hand in the air while she waited for the words to come. 'We met…earlier…on the jetty.'

If it were possible, his face got even more thunderous. 'Heather! I've told you never to—'

'God! Take a chill pill, Luke. I was only crabbing!' Then she spun on her heel and stomped off again. Luke looked as if he'd been slapped in the face. Gaby swallowed.

He slumped down on a chair and rubbed his face. The start of his next sentence was muffled by his hands. 'I don't know how much Mrs Pullman told you, but we're facing a rather difficult set of circumstances with Heather.' He looked up at her, his eyes pleading. 'Please, don't let that little outburst put you off. She's a good kid underneath it all. But she's had a lot to deal with in the last few years.'

Gaby smiled gently at him. 'It's okay. I know about the trial and…everything.'

Luke let out a long breath. He seemed very

relieved not to have to run through the details.
'Good. If that hasn't put you off, I don't know what
will.'

'Oh, I—'

He didn't seem to hear her.

'She took her mother's death very hard. And then
she had to deal with me being…away. We've only
been living together again for a couple of months,
so we're still getting to know each other again,
really.' He looked down at the table, as if he hadn't
meant to say all of that in front of her.

The silence stretched. If only there were something to say, something she could do to make it all
go away. This was the point at which her alarm bells
should be ringing. That little tug at her heartstrings
always meant trouble. She'd promised herself she
wouldn't fall completely in love with her charge
again this time.

If getting inside a child's mind was her strength,
the fact she let them too far into her heart was her
weakness. Too many times she'd been left heart-
broken when a family moved overseas or didn't need
her any more.

She was older and wiser now; she should be past
this. And maybe, if David hadn't kept putting off the
issue of children, she would have been. It was
probably down to the overly-loud ticking of her bio-
logical clock that she was ignoring all the old
warning signals. If she had any sense, she would
excuse herself and return to London—leave this

family to someone who could look at them objectively, help them without getting too emotionally involved. It would be better for Luke and Heather in the long run too.

'I'd better go and see to my errant daughter.' He pushed the chair back and stood up.

He looked so lost, so unsure of what to do, that Gaby put a hand on his arm to stall him. 'Let me go.' The least she could do before she left was help defuse the current situation.

He started to shake his head, but then he said, 'Okay. Heather's room is on the left at the top of the stairs.'

She crept up the stairs, stood outside the door, took a deep breath and knocked gently.

'Go away! I don't want to speak to you!'

'Heather? It's me—Gaby.'

'Oh.'

'Can I come in?'

The door edged open and Heather poked her nose in the gap. 'It's a bit messy.'

Gaby smiled. 'I wouldn't worry about that. You should have seen my room when I was your age. My mum used to have an awful go at me. In the end I just shoved it all in the cupboard and hoped no one opened the door. If they had, they would have been buried in an avalanche of clothes and toys!'

Heather gasped and her eyes got even bigger and rounder.

'Believe it, kid, you've got nothing on me.'

The door swung wide and Gaby walked in. She

32   HER PARENTHOOD ASSIGNMENT

perched on the edge of a bed decked in pink and
frilly bed-clothes. Heather grimaced. 'He thinks I'm
still a baby.'

'I'm sure he doesn't think you're a baby. He was
probably trying very hard to make things nice for
you.'

Heather made a gagging noise and rolled her eyes,
but when her face returned to normal her expression
had softened. 'Are you really going to be my nanny?'

'Well—'

'I don't need looking after, you know. I'm all
right on my own.'

Did no one in this house ever let you finish a
sentence?

She swivelled to face Heather. 'I know that. But
your dad has to have someone in the house while
he's out at work. He's not allowed to leave you
alone, you know.'

''Spose so.'

'Why don't we go downstairs and chat to your
dad about it?'

'*You* can talk to him, if you like.'

It might have sounded as if Heather were reluctant to make peace with her father, but Gaby saw the
ache in her eyes. She desperately wanted to be able
to open up to him; she just didn't know how. What
had it been like for her while her father had been in
prison? How often had she seen him? Had she been
carted along in her best dress and told to tell him she
was being a good girl?

No wonder they couldn't communicate with each other. They'd probably spent years being on their best behaviour, each making sure the other didn't know how they were suffering.

When they reached the kitchen, Luke was so surprised his mouth dropped open. Gaby thought it was a shame he recovered quickly. Too quickly. It would have done Heather good to see the look on his face—that same aching expression she'd been wearing just moments before.

Heather opened the fridge door and stuck her head inside. 'I'm hungry.'

Luke looked at Heather and then at Gaby. 'Would you like to stay for dinner? It would be a good chance to get to know us better. Start afresh.'

She was going to decline, say she needed to get back to her car, but she saw Heather's face above the fridge door and stopped short. The girl's eyes were wide, as if she were waiting for something important, like the results of a spelling test. When Gaby nodded, she glowed.

'Heather, why don't you show Gaby the house, while I get the food ready?'

Heather let the fridge door swing closed and tugged Gaby by the hand.

'Come on. I'll show you the terrace. It's cool.'

Gaby thought the terrace was way more than cool. The flat roof above the kitchen had been turned into a seating area with railings and a stunning view of the River Dart. The light was fading and a gold sun glowed through dense grey clouds. Gaby breathed in the salty air. She could tell it was only a couple of miles to the estuary.

The terrace could be reached directly from two of the bedrooms on the first floor: the master bedroom, which she didn't look in—it felt too much like snooping—and a guest bedroom. A flight of stairs led down to the kitchen door, making it a great place to have breakfast when the weather improved.

She went still. It looked as if her subconscious was already planning on staying, whether the rest of her liked it or not. That wasn't a good sign.

The rest of the house was just as impressive. It had an unusual layout and a kind of quirky charm. The best feature by far was the little area just outside the back door. A flight of steps led down to a flat area with rings to tie boats to. At that moment the tide was out and she could see more steps that led down on to the stony beach. But when the tide was up, you could row right up to it and skip straight into the house—like Venice!

Gaby frowned. Another rogue thought of her ex intruded. The only time she'd been to Venice had been with David. He'd liked the first-class holidays and exotic destinations. Although she suspected it was more for the dinner party stories he could tell later, than for the experience itself. He hadn't stopped moaning the week they'd stayed in Venice; it had sucked all the joy out of it for her.

Both Gaby and Heather didn't need to be called when dinner was ready. Smells were emanating from the kitchen and Gaby's tummy suddenly rumbled. She hadn't stopped to eat on the journey down here—not even a plastic sandwich at a service station. She'd been too intent on making it to Lower Hadwell before dark.

They arrived back in the kitchen just in time to see Luke slapping pizza slices on to plates. Her appetite took a nosedive. It looked like the worst sort of convenience food. Luke and Heather didn't seem to mind. They attacked their share with relish.

Gaby gingerly put a slice to her lips. Anaemic cheese and a cardboard base. Yuck! Still, she wasn't going to be rude. She took as big a bite as she dared and chewed the minimum amount of times before swallowing.

'Is there any salad?'

Two pairs of eyes locked on to her. She might as well have asked them if they wanted a side order of slugs. Vegetables were obviously a foreign concept in this household.

'Never mind. This is…lovely.'

She looked out of the window to try and take her mind off the artificial taste. The sky was a beautiful slate-blue. It was getting quite dark. Suddenly she stopped chewing and scanned the kitchen for a wall clock.

She gulped down her mouthful. 'What time is it?'

Luke looked at his watch. 'Just gone six.'

Drat! Just when she'd thought the day couldn't get any more complicated.

'Is something the matter?'

'I think I just missed the last ferry.'

Luke put his pizza slice down. 'You came over on the ferry?'

'I left my car across the river.' She stood up. 'It's a long story. I'm not very good with… If I run, do you think I can catch the ferry guy?'

She started off in search of her shoes. Luke followed her into what Heather had called the 'mud room' during their tour.

'It's too late. Ben will be in the Ferryboat Inn by now and the only thing that'll move him is the bell for last orders.'

Gaby dropped her face into her hands and massaged the kinks out of her forehead. 'Today was not supposed to be like this!' Her return to being a nanny was going to be marked by a new, calm professionalism. Not ferries and mud and little girls with big round eyes. Suddenly everything felt so tangled and messy.

Luke's voice was taut. 'Are you saying you don't want the job?'

'Yes!…No. I mean, I'm not sure I'm what you and Heather are looking for. I need time to think.'

Silence.

Her hands dropped to her sides. He was staring at her, but he didn't look angry, he just looked… defeated.

'Of course, I understand your decision. Not everyone is comfortable taking on a family with a history like ours. That narrowed down the candidates considerably in the first place.' He swallowed. 'Heather will just have to go and stay with her grand-parents while I sort something out.'

Now it was her turn to swallow. The look on his face was all her fault.

'Are you sure you can't stay, Gaby? I know it might not look like it, but Heather has taken a shine to you. She didn't manage to speak at all to the other interviewees. She just grunted and tried to evaporate them with her laser vision.'

Gaby let out a little giggle. Luke seemed com-pletely taken aback, as if he'd forgotten he could be funny and had just surprised himself. She put a hand over her mouth and tried to stifle her growing smile. It was no good. The smile accel-erated into a laugh.

'I can just see it!' she blurted between giggles. 'Heather plotting to put crabs in their beds...'

And then Luke was laughing too. That was all she needed. It started her off again. And while she leant against the wall for support, her mind drifted free and she wondered if this was the same kind of hys-terical laughter that attacked people at funerals, because there truly wasn't anything to laugh about.

The laughter finally ebbed away and they stood there looking at each other in the gathering gloom. Luke sobered.

'It's a pity. I have the feeling you could be very good for us...for Heather, I mean.'

Gaby felt her heart beating in her chest and knew she was going to say something truly stupid.

'I'll do it. I'll take the job.'

CHAPTER THREE

LUKE checked the digital clock on the oven. Five forty-five. Much too early to make breakfast, or wake Heather, or do anything else he could think of to fill the time. He carefully opened the kitchen door and went outside.

It was dark, really dark. He still hadn't got used to that. In prison, there had always been the harsh yellow glow of a bulb somewhere. Always a clang, or a hum, or a shout to break the silence.

Here on the river it was completely still. The water was glassy and inky black, reflecting the myriad stars above. On a clear night here you couldn't even see the main constellations, there were so many stars in the sky. Like now, he could see the dusty sweep of the Milky Way and, if he kept really still, sometimes he could see a satellite cutting its way through the overcrowded sky in a clean even line.

He shivered and looked back at the water. He couldn't spend too long watching the sky when it was like this. It felt too big.

If only he could sleep better. It might stop him feeling as if he had to hold himself together, as if the world had too many possibilities and he had to stop himself from thinking about all the choices, the different avenues life could take. Right now he had to concentrate on being still, on being solid. On being someone Heather could depend on.

Having Gaby here was going to help. He looked up at the guest room windows and envied the long, unbroken sleep she was having. There had been nothing for it but to have her stay the night. Her car was the other side of the river and there was nowhere to stay in the village. He supposed she would have to return home and collect some things before she moved in full time.

Thank heavens she'd changed her mind at the last minute. He was starting work at the medical centre next week and, if he hadn't managed to sort something out, Heather would have had to stay with Lucy's parents again, and then they'd be back to square one.

Since it was low tide again, he went down the steps outside the kitchen and on to the beach, careful to keep close to the house so the lights from the kitchen gave him some idea of where he was treading.

Heather had changed so much in the last few years. When he'd left, she'd been in her first year of school. Her uniform had been too big and Lucy always used to do her hair in cute little bunches.

Lucy's parents had brought her to see him on

visiting days and he'd seen her change over the years. Not smoothly and slowly, hardly noticing the little differences, but in fits and starts, like flicking through a series of snapshots. He smiled when he thought of the time she'd arrived and shown him her first missing tooth, announcing proudly, 'Look Daddy, my tongue has a window!'

Over time, the gaps between visits had got longer. Her grandparents had begun to send notes saying it was upsetting Heather too much to come and see him. They thought she needed to have a normal life, as much as possible. And, in their book, seeing your father across a dingy prison table, being artificially bright and pretending nothing was wrong, was obviously *not* normal. Hell, it wasn't even normal in his book.

He picked up a handful of small flat stones and concentrated on throwing them into the water. The reflected stars distorted and scurried away. He kept throwing until the light turned a milky grey and the thoughts he didn't want to stir were lying at the bottom of the river with the pebbles.

Gaby could see him out there on the beach—a dark figure, barely visible in the dull glow of the kitchen lights. What on earth must he have gone through to make him turn out like this? It didn't bear thinking about.

But she would have to face it sooner or later, because she was pretty sure she wasn't going to be able to help Heather unless she helped Luke first. In her experience, the parents often needed training more than the children did.

She walked away from the window and got back into bed. The sheets were still warm and she snuggled down and thought about the future. Luke seemed to want her to start as soon as possible. And since she was here—with a bag packed for a week— and she'd started to bond with Heather, it seemed daft to leave so soon.

She could always go and visit Caroline in a couple of weeks. Now she'd be closer, she could go for the weekend or something.

She rolled over and tried to ignore the fact she was already making little sacrifices for this family, already putting their needs before her own. It always started this way…

'I don't want to go to Jodi's to play! I hate her.'

Heather's voice was clearly recognisable through the closed guest room door. Gaby tried not to listen as she brushed her hair, but there wasn't much chance of escaping the exchange between father and daughter.

'It'll be good for you to get to know some of your classmates better. You've been there half a term and you haven't made any friends.'

'Good for who? You just don't want me here!'

'Heather! You know that's not true!'

The only answer Luke got was the slam of Heather's bedroom door.

Gaby closed her eyes. She felt like collecting her car this morning, then driving back to London at eighty miles an hour, without stopping. She wanted to tell Luke she couldn't take the job after all. It was all too close, too raw. What if she couldn't do this?

But if she left, Heather and Luke would be separated again and their relationship might not survive. The thought that she might be able to turn the tide and see father and daughter happy together made her wrap all of her own feelings of insecurity in a bundle and pack them away somewhere dark inside herself.

Luke had offered her a lift down to the village to get her car. Not because it was too far to walk, but because it was drizzling on and off and her most sensible shoes were still slightly damp from the day before.

When Gaby got outside, Heather was already in the back seat of the Range Rover, arms folded and looking as if she were willing it to sink into the mud. Luke locked up the house, opened the driver's door and got in without a word.

She turned to smile at her charge and Heather rolled her eyes. Gaby pressed her lips together to stop herself smiling. She wasn't going to encourage Heather to be cheeky, but she was glad the girl saw her as an ally, not another enemy.

It was only a matter of minutes before the Range Rover had ploughed through the muddy lane and arrived in the village. Luke pulled in near to the jetty to let Gaby out.

'Just out of interest, why exactly did you leave

your car over the other side of the river and get the ferry over?'

Gaby shuffled in her seat and bent to pick her handbag up from the footwell. 'Well…it's a little difficult to drive and navigate at the same time in these lanes.'

'In other words, you got lost.'

'No! Well, just a bit. I was following directions for Lower Hadwell. I just didn't notice the little boat on the signs.'

Luke sighed. It was a world-weary noise that said *typical* very eloquently. Why couldn't he just laugh at her, like the ferryman had? She could handle that. He shook his head and pulled out of the parking place.

Where were they going now?

Obviously Luke had made an executive decision of some kind and didn't think it was worth discussing with a dimwit like her. She was tempted to roll her eyes *à la* Heather, but she just clutched her handbag with rather more force than necessary and looked out of the window. They were climbing up the steep hill that led out of the village.

'Where are we going? I need to get my car.'

Luke didn't bother looking at her when he replied. In fact, it seemed as if he was taking it as a personal affront that she should dare ask. 'I'm going to drop Heather off at Jodi Allford's, then we are going to get the ferry and fetch your car round.'

'We?'

'I don't want my new nanny ending up in Cornwall when I need her here.'

She glanced across to see if that was a joke. His mouth was set in a hard line.

He was treating her like a child! And if this was only a fraction of what he dished out to Heather, she could see why father and daughter were getting along so famously. Talk about a complete sense of humour failure!

But then, this man didn't have a lot to smile about. Her fingers loosened their grip on her innocent bag. She wasn't being fair.

'Are you going to navigate, then?'

'That's the plan. Don't worry. You're not putting me out. We'll pass through Totnes and I was intending to go to the bank there this morning anyway.'

Her put him out!

Old resentments bubbled below the surface. She did not need another man treating her as if she only had one brain cell. She slumped down into her seat and fumed. No *would you mind if I came along…?* or *what do you think if…?* She ought to tell him to drive himself to the flipping bank. She could do just fine on her own.

Instead she just nodded and said, 'Okay.'

Then she rolled her eyes at herself. Why did she always do this? Swallow what she really wanted to say and give the nice, polite, *acceptable* answer?

That little exchange set the tone for the whole journey. Luke merely nodded at Ben, the ferryman, when they hopped aboard his little boat, and he hadn't said much more than 'next left' and 'second exit' since they'd driven away from the quay in her battered old car.

There was hardly any traffic in the lanes this time of year and Gaby had time to let her mind wander. What was wrong with Luke this morning? Yesterday evening, once the storm with Heather had blown over, he'd been polite and, while not chatty, she'd thought they'd begun to form an acceptable sort of working relationship. Even outbursts of frustration were better than this stony silence. He seemed so distant.

'Straight on at the crossroads.'

There it was again! That little edge in his voice that made it seem like an order and not a request. As she slowed to wait at the junction, she looked sideways at him. His face was blank and he was staring straight ahead.

At least he wasn't criticising her driving. David had always had something to say about how fast she was going. Well, how slow, to be exact. He always had an opinion on how things ought to be done. But he'd seemed so charming and knowledgeable in the early days of their relationship—and she'd been so young—that she'd deferred to him on everything. He'd been her husband, after all, and she'd wanted to make him happy.

A little dig here, a cutting remark there, and David had moulded her into the image of the perfect corporate wife. And the really tragic thing was she'd let him, without hesitation or question, because she'd been so stupidly grateful a dashing young banker like him had even looked at her, let alone wanted to marry her.

She suspected now he'd just seen her as a blank canvas. And when they'd separated she'd gone about changing herself, scrubbing away the traces of his influence on her.

She'd lost quite a bit of weight. That had given her a grim satisfaction. David had always made little remarks about how she should get down the gym more. And now she dressed how she wanted to dress, in comfortable clothes, not a designer label or a gold earring in sight.

She had never really loved him, she knew that now. She'd just been so terrified of losing him that she'd erased her own personality. And, in doing so, she'd paved the path to rejection herself. He'd run off with Cara, a career woman, who was exciting and intelligent and unconventional… All the things she wasn't, according to David.

She'd become a suburban version of Frankenstein's monster. A patchwork person, put together with all the right bits in the right places, but somehow the life—the spirit—had been missing.

Luke's voice boomed in her ear. 'I said, "Get into the right-hand lane."'

'What?' She came to and realised they'd reached the outskirts of a town. 'Sorry. Must have drifted off.' She didn't look at him, but she could tell he was giving her a long hard stare. When he thought he'd made his point, he folded his arms and looked straight ahead.

She turned right, following his directions, and managed to park near the town centre without further embarrassment. Luke unfolded his long frame from the passenger seat and got out, slamming the door as he did so. When she'd finished untangling her handbag strap from around the gear stick and joined him, she found him staring down the street.

'I'll meet you back here in half an hour,' he said and marched off without looking back.

He walked into the car park and spotted her leaning against the car, a crowd of shopping bags at her feet. She looked like so many of the other shoppers in her jeans and hooded jacket. If he hadn't been looking out for her, he probably wouldn't have given her a second glance. She looked quite ordinary.

But he *was* looking out for her. And, as he looked more closely, he noticed something. Even without make-up and her hair scragged into a ponytail, she looked fresh and vibrant—not in the same way as Lucy, who'd been packed so full of restless energy she had hardly been able to contain it—but in the sense that she seemed full of untapped potential. On the cusp of something. He envied her that.

He'd expected to shed the sense of hopelessness with the regulation uniform when he'd walked out the prison gates. But it still weighed him down and he didn't know how to shake it off. And now, here was this woman doing it all so effortlessly. He wasn't sure whether he was fascinated or frustrated.

She turned to him as he neared the car and he said something—anything—to hide his confusion. 'What have you got in those? Clothes?'

'Food.'

'But we don't need any—'

'Luke, I looked in your freezer this morning. It's full of cardboard boxes and shrink-wrapped nasties. It's about time you and Heather ate something with nutrients in it. Goodness knows, it might improve both your moods.'

Luke was about to protest that his mood was just fine, thank you very much, but then he remembered how tightly clenched his intestines were all the time and how Heather just had to give him one of her glares and his head would swim with the effort of keeping a lid on his temper.

He grunted and saw a small smile appear on Gaby's lips.

'Just you wait. Your taste buds will sing.'

'Pretty full of yourself, aren't you?'

Still, she was probably right. The food *inside* had been even worse than the contents of his freezer. In comparison, the ready meals tasted like ambrosia. Perhaps he shouldn't have subjected his growing daughter to such a limited diet.

'I didn't hire you to cook, you know. I'm not paying you any extra.'

'I like cooking. And besides you *did* hire me to look after Heather. And I feel I would be failing miserably if I let her eat fast food and junk all day long.'

'I've looked after Heather just fine up until now, thank you.'

'I didn't mean…'

She rummaged in her pockets and pulled out the car keys. He watched her unlock the car, shaking her head as she did so, obviously deciding it wasn't worth the effort to answer him.

He picked up the shopping bags and put them in the boot. He hadn't meant to bite her head off like that. It was just that *he* should have thought of the quality of the food he was giving his daughter, not left it up to a stranger who'd been in their lives less than twenty-four hours. It was just another area he was failing in.

He wanted to say sorry, but the words wouldn't come. Too many years of burying all sense of civility had left their toll on him. It had been too dangerous to show any sign of weakness, so he'd had to act tough to survive. He'd blithely thought that, once he was home, he'd be able to flick a switch and return to the man he'd once been, but it wasn't that simple. What had once been a choice had now become a habit.

As they climbed in the car and drove away, he looked across at Gaby. Two little creases had appeared between her eyebrows while she concentrated on the winding roads. He sighed and scrubbed his face with his hands. He'd been like a bear with a sore head this morning and she'd just taken it. No screaming, no temper tantrums. She seemed to understand that he was struggling with a new addition to the household and gave him space accordingly.

He cranked the handle by his side to open the window a little. The air was cold and very fresh, but he needed a break from the smell of her. Nothing fancy. No perfume or expensive cosmetics, just the scent of a clean woman. A good woman. She had to be a saint to take his family on. And perhaps this good woman could help him remember how to be a good father. Once it had been so effortless.

But that was the problem. He wanted Gaby here for all the obvious practical reasons, but a part of him was resisting her presence. There was something about her that eroded his barriers while he didn't even notice. He'd laughed with her. Had actually laughed. He'd opened up with her. Those kinds of things were dangerous. If he didn't look out his iron-plating would buckle and then he'd lose control—and that would be no good at all for Heather.

However much this Gaby made him want to breathe out and smile, he had to resist it.

'Next left.'

Gaby didn't move.

'Gaby, I said next left! Now look… We've gone past the turning. You'll have to stop in the passing place up ahead, then go back.'

He watched her fingers tighten over the gear stick and she jerked it into place. His eyes widened slightly.

So, he was getting to her. Perhaps she wasn't as *au fait* with his sore-headed-bear routine as he'd thought. Well, good! It would be easier to keep her at arm's length that way. Then he wouldn't be bothered by her clean smell and the warmth in her eyes.

CHAPTER FOUR

A LASAGNE was bubbling away in the oven. Gaby fished her mobile phone out of her pocket and dialled a number while she had a spare minute.

'Hello, Mum. It's me.'

'Good grief, Gabrielle. What are you doing calling at this hour? You know we always sit down to dinner at six-thirty sharp. Your father will only get difficult if his soup goes cold.'

'Sorry, Mum. This won't take long.'

'Well? What's the emergency?'

'I just wanted to let you know that I'm going to be away for a while.'

'Oh, good heavens! You're not going on holiday with that Jules you share a flat with, are you? She seems the sort to get into trouble in a foreign country, if you ask me. Always got too much flesh on display.'

Gaby closed her eyes, took a deep breath and answered. 'No, Mum. I'm not going away with Jules.'

'Just as well. I don't know, Gabrielle. Your father

and I didn't raise you to go gallivanting off at the drop of a hat. I just don't know what to think since you broke it off with David.'

'Mum, David was the one who—'

'Well, that's beside the point, isn't it? I don't know why you can't make another go of it—let bygones be bygones. Goodness knows, your brother and Hattie have had their problems, but they've been able to make it work. Look at them now, two lovely boys and another baby on the way. You're running out of time, you know, if you want a family. And at your age it's going to be hard to find a nice man to take you on with all your history.'

Gaby tuned her mother out and made the appropriate noises at the appropriate moments. Why did every conversation always end up with her mother pointing out that she wasn't making a success of her life like her golden-boy brother? Next to him she just felt ordinary.

Once her mother had given up on her following Justin to Cambridge, she'd hatched a plan to train her up as a nanny and pack her off to look after Lord and Lady So-and-so's kids. What a coup that had been at her afternoon teas.

Gaby sighed. She'd done everything she could to make her parents proud of her, but it was never good enough. She even wondered whether one of the reasons she'd married David, one of Justin's university buddies, had just been so she could bask in some of the reflected glory.

She was jerked back to the present by the raised pitch in her mother's voice. 'I'm going to have to dash. Your father has just started bellowing.'

'Bye, Mum. Send my love to—'

But her mother had rung off. Gaby walked over to the fridge, still staring at her phone. Her mother hadn't even asked where she was going, or how long for. She popped the phone back in her jeans pocket and got on with making the salad dressing. There was a creak by the door as she measured out the vinegar.

Luke.

She wasn't sure how she knew it was him, she just sensed it. She carried on pouring the oil into the dressing mixture and waited for him to say something. The fine hairs on the back of her neck started to lift and she became so self-conscious she whisked the dressing into a tornado.

In the end, she couldn't stand it any more and she turned slowly. Her eyes met his.

'Is there anything I can do to help, Gaby?'

She shook her head. 'No. It's just about ready. You could call Heather, though, if you like?'

He just stood in the doorway and kept looking at her. She looked back, doing her best not to fidget. And then he disappeared without saying anything. A shadow seemed to hover in the doorway where he'd been standing, as if the intensity of his presence had left an imprint in the air. The whisk in her hand was hanging in mid-air, dripping dressing on the floor. She quickly plopped it back in the jug and reached for the kitchen towel.

By the time Luke returned with Heather, the lasagne was on the table and Gaby was ready and waiting with an oven mitt in one hand and a serving spoon in the other. Heather slid into a seat and eyed the serving dish suspiciously. Gaby gave her a small portion, then spooned a generous helping on to a plate for Luke.

She waited, eyebrows raised and spoon poised to cut through the pasta, waiting for him to signal if he wanted more. He nodded so enthusiastically that Gaby couldn't help but smile as she dolloped another spoonful on to his plate and passed it across.

'Do start,' she said, serving herself.

The Armstrongs weren't ones to stand on ceremony, it seemed. Both Luke and Heather started to demolish their dinner without further hesitation. Gaby, however, took her time and watched. She tried with difficulty to keep the corners of her mouth from turning up as Luke closed his eyes and let out a small growl of pleasure. It was the first time she'd seen him genuinely forget his troubles and live in the moment.

She shook her head and stared at her own plate. Get real, Gaby! A nice lasagne is hardly going to undo five years of emotional torment. But when she looked up at Luke and Heather, both on the verge of clearing their plates, she couldn't help feeling just a little triumphant.

'This is even better than Granny's,' said Heather, her mouth only half empty before she shoved in another forkful.

'I thought you were boasting this afternoon, but you were right. My taste buds are serenading you. Where on earth did you learn to cook like this?'

Gaby flushed with stupid pride. Luke's approval shouldn't matter. He was talking about her cooking, not passing judgement on her as a person. She really needed to calm down. 'Just cooking courses at the local adult education college.'

Six of them. Including the Cordon Bleu one. David had insisted. He'd liked the idea of hosting dinner parties for his business associates. But he'd never savoured her food the way Luke was doing now, as if every bite was a small piece of heaven. Perhaps their marriage would have been salvageable if he had, but everything had been too salty, lumpy or cold for David.

Not for the first time, she sighed with relief that catering to David's fussy eating habits was now Cara's job. Or perhaps it wasn't. She doubted that Superwoman did anything as mundane as cooking. The thought of David tucking into a plastic-wrapped meal with his silver-plated cutlery made her feel strangely warm inside.

A small smile still lingered on her face as she started to stack the plates at the end of the meal. This kitchen seemed warm and inviting and cooking for Luke and Heather had been a joy. She'd thought she'd be treading on eggshells while she stayed at the Old Boathouse, but it all felt very natural.

She balanced the plates on top of the serving dish and picked the pile up, only to find Luke step towards her and place his hands over the top of hers. The tingle where their fingers made contact was unexpected—so unexpected that her smile flickered out and she stared hard at the pile of dishes and tangle of fingers. They both went very still.

The tingling got worse and she gripped harder.

'Thank you, Gaby. I really appreciate you doing that for us. It was the best meal I've had in a long time.'

Now pins and needles were travelling right up her arms until they broke through her skin in big pink blotches on her neck. She could feel it. That always happened when she was...

'I'll do the dishes,' he said, giving the stack a little tug.

She nodded her response. The words wouldn't come.

He smiled. 'You need to let go of the plates, then.'

'Of course.' But her fingers were blatantly ignoring his very logical suggestion. 'I'll make the coffee.'

Then, before she knew it, fingers and dishes were whisked away. She wiped the remnants of the tingles away on the front of her jeans.

'How do you take it?' she asked him as the last of the plates were being stacked on the rack and the kettle was bubbling madly.

Luke dried his hands and looked over his shoulder. 'Black, one sugar.'

The same as she did.

Somewhere inside, all the silliness to do with plates and fingers and lasagne and *black with one sugar* consolidated into a glow in the pit of her stomach. She tried to quench it, but the embers warmed her all the same.

She handed Luke his coffee and started to walk out of the room with her own.

'Gaby?'

She turned.

'Aren't you going to stay and drink it in here?'

'Um. No. I've got…things I need to do. Upstairs.' She looked up at the ceiling and caught her breath. 'I'll see you in the morning, Luke. I think I need an early night.'

He sat down at the table and supported his chin with his hand.

'Okay, then,' he said, breaking eye contact. 'I'll see you tomorrow.'

Gaby took a short trip back to London the next weekend to collect more of her things, and to let Jules know she wouldn't need her spare room for a while. Jules was a friend from her art classes at the adult education centre.

She'd been lovely while the divorce had been going through and had offered Gaby her spare room when the marital home had been sold and Gaby had needed somewhere to stay while she'd looked for something more permanent.

She suspected she'd been cramping her flatmate's style recently. Jules had just started dating a guy she'd had a crush on for months, and would probably be glad of the extra privacy.

Since most of Gaby's larger possessions were already in storage, it was just a case of packing a couple of bags and she'd be ready to go. She was just stuffing the last few bits into a holdall when the phone rang.

'Hello?'

'Gabrielle?'

'Mum!'

'I thought you were going away with that Jules person.'

'No, Mum. I—' Hang on a second. 'Why are you calling if you thought I'd be away?'

'It's obvious, dear. I was going to leave a message on your answer phone about Justin's birthday for when you get back.'

'Justin's birthday,' she said slowly. That wasn't for another two months.

'Just so you don't double-book yourself.'

Of course. Harriet was having one of her big parties, but then Harriet always made a fuss about Justin's birthday.

'Well, Mum, I've got a new job. I'm not sure I'm going to—'

'Don't be ridiculous! You can't miss your own

brother's party. It's the sixteenth, dear. Are you writing it down?'

'Of course, I am,' Gaby replied, looking at the pad on her beside table and doing nothing to move towards it.

'I'll be in touch in a few weeks to fill you in on all the details. Bye now.'

Then all Gaby could hear was the dial tone purring in her ear.

Luke tugged frantically on the strings of the kite, but it was too late. It fell out of the air and crashed on to the deserted beach. He sighed and trudged towards it. Gaby might be a bit of a shrinking violet at times, but she could talk an Eskimo into buying snow, and what was more, he'd love her for it!

This outing to the beach with Heather had been her idea.

You're not working this Sunday, she'd said. The weather report says it's going to be sunny but windy, she'd said. Great weather for flying kites. Heather would love it…

And before he knew it, he was buying a multi-coloured contraption in town and spending his Sunday afternoon watching it nosedive into the shingle again and again.

Heather had lost interest after ten minutes. So now he was left to keep up the pretence while she and Gaby wandered along the shore, arm in arm, and collected shells and bits of quartz.

He stopped to watch them. They were deep in conversation, sharing girl-type secrets, no doubt. His heart squeezed a little. Gaby had made such a difference to their home in the last three weeks. He still had to duck when Heather was in a foul mood, but more and more she was laughing and smiling, and he'd even caught her singing to herself.

He could see glimpses of the happy little girl she'd once been. That same cheeky smile she'd had, aged three, when she knew she'd said something funny or cute. The way she stroked a strand of her own hair when she was tired.

And it was all down to Gaby. He couldn't take credit for the tiniest bit of it. All he managed was to stretch his mouth into a smile when it was required, and to say the right things—as if he were reading from a script—and watch his daughter blossom.

Gaby was getting closer and closer to Heather and, miracle of miracles, Heather was letting her.

And, all the while, he stayed on the fringes and watched. He was just as much on the outside of his daughter's life as he'd been all those years behind bars. Why he couldn't work his way into the centre—where all the laughter and warmth was—was more than he could fathom.

He watched as Gaby and Heather broke into a run and chased each other along the edge of the surf. The wind was cold and it blew their scarves in front of their faces, which only made them laugh all the more.

How did she do it?

The woman he'd thought at first seemed ordinary, nothing special, had the ability to reach out to a heart and see it respond. A very rare thing indeed. He caught himself studying her, trying to work out what her secret was, where all that warmth and courage came from.

He alternated between admiring her and hating her for it.

He tore his gaze away and returned it to the kite lying a short distance away on the small round pebbles. It seemed injured, lying there fluttering half-heartedly. He walked over and surveyed it with dismay.

The two figures walking along the shore hadn't even seen it crash.

It was all in a tangle and he didn't know what to do with it.

Heather sat in the passenger seat of Gaby's car and fiddled with the catch on the glove compartment.

'Come on, Heather. You're going to be late if you don't actually get out of the car and walk through the gates.'

Heather grimaced and opened and shut the glove compartment a few more times. 'Twenty' she said, casting Gaby a weary look.

Okay. Heather was taking a cryptic tack again. Gaby was getting used to this. Heather had problems expressing her fears. Rather than blurting out how she felt, she would leave a trail of crumbs, making her interrogator work for answers she was actually desperate to give. But they didn't have time for this; the school bell was going to ring in less than a minute.

'Twenty what, Heather?' Twenty more slams of the glove box and the whole car would fall apart? She took hold of Heather's hand gently and removed it from the glove box catch. Heather pulled her hand away and tucked it under the school bag on her lap.

'Twenty school days until the Easter break.'

Gaby's heart went out to her, it really did, but she could see where Heather was going with this, and there was no way she was going to let the girl manipulate her. She was going to school today, and that was that.

'It won't be as bad as you think, sweetheart.'

'How would you know? It was probably at least a hundred years since you were at school! You don't know anything about it. Nobody does.'

Heather was giving her what Gaby always referred to as a *laser vision* stare— thanks to Luke's apt description. She refused to take the bait, especially now she'd worked out that Heather created conflict when she didn't get her own way. So she leaned across, pulled the handle and opened the door for her.

'Come on, miss. Out. One foot in front of the other, walk through the door, sit your bottom on a chair and stay there. It's not hard. And then, when you come out again, it'll be nineteen days and counting.'

Heather flounced from the car, as only a disgruntled pre-teen could, dragging her bag behind her.

'I'll see you after netball practice,' Gaby yelled

after her. But Heather was too busy ploughing a path though her schoolmates to hear.

She pulled the door closed and started the car. Heather was making progress, but there was still a long way to go. She and Luke were enjoying a turbulent truce. They still didn't know how to resolve their differences when a spat erupted, but at least in the in-between times she could see they were both trying.

Although she was very fond of Heather, she was determined to keep a professional distance. There were so many reasons why she couldn't afford to lose her heart to this needy little girl and her silently aching father.

Distance. That was what they all needed. Luke certainly needed time and space to sort himself out. At least, that was the reason she gave herself for keeping out of his way in the evenings, and always, always leaving the dinner plates on the table for him to clear away.

Back at the Old Boathouse, she parked her car near the back door and let herself in. Seven and a half hours until she had to pick Heather up. It seemed an awfully long time. But she had a shopping list to write and she might as well check whether Heather had put her school uniform from last week in the laundry basket, rather than stuffing it under her bed.

By noon her shopping list was written in a small neat hand and every last sock of Heather's had been accounted for and deposited in the washing machine.

The beds were made, a pot of home-made soup sat bubbling on the hob and she had organised the contents of the freezer.

She sat at the spotlessly clean kitchen table and stared out of the window. It was a typically grey March day. Even so, the colours on the river here were wonderful. Steel greys, mossy greens and slate blues. And the light!

There was inspiration everywhere you looked, no matter the time of day or the weather. When she was younger, she'd have been out there on the beach, brush in hand, like a shot.

Gaby sat up a little straighter.

Why not? What was there to stop her? She'd missed the watercolour classes she'd taken while married to David. Since the divorce she'd had neither the time nor the money to lavish on things like that. But with Heather in school most of the week, she'd have plenty of time to unearth a talent she thought she'd buried for good, and still get all her work done. She jumped up, grabbed her keys and drove into town grinning all the way.

Down a cobbled street she found a shop selling art supplies. She emerged with a carrier bag full of paint tubes, brushes, paper and her head full of ideas for her first project.

She wandered through the town without really paying attention to where she was going and found herself in Bayard's Cove, a little dead end street near the ferry. One side was open to the river, and a squat, ruined turret of an old fort built to guard the estuary sat where the road ended.

She dipped down and entered the fort through its low doorway. A row of arched windows framed the view up to Dartmouth Castle on the rolling headland.

She would just fit nicely in one of those arches, she decided. Soon her legs were dangling over the ledge, the water lapping below. She pulled a sketch pad and pencil out of her shopping bag and set to work capturing what she saw: bulbous clouds pushing across the sky like an armada, sail boats criss-crossing the water and the higgledy-piggledy houses of Kingswear on the other side of the river.

This was heaven. It had been so long since she'd done something just for her own pleasure. What started out as a quick sketch, rapidly grew in scale and detail. It was only when she glanced up and noticed the light was starting to fade that she checked her watch. Four o'clock. She had time to head home, drop off her bags, then run up to collect Heather from netball practice.

She took a second to consider her sketch, then flipped the pad closed, praying the traffic warden hadn't slapped a ticket on her windscreen while she'd been sketching.

When she returned to the Old Boathouse, she was surprised to see Luke's car parked at an angle in the lane. He wasn't due home until at least seven o'clock. She wanted to show him what she'd been up to, so she fished the pad out of her bag as she walked up to the back door. Once in the mud room, she called out, 'Hi there! What are you doing back so—?'

The look on Luke's face as she entered the lounge brought her up short.

'Where the hell have you been?'

CHAPTER FIVE

Was he yelling at *her?*

Gaby took a quick look over her shoulder, just to double-check no one had walked in behind her, but they were alone in the room.

'Well? Where have you been?'

Her fingers twitched as she waited for her voice to work. She waved the pad a fraction of an inch. 'I've been sketching…'

Her voice trailed off. He'd lost his rag with Heather over the last few weeks, but never had she seen this kind of raw fury in his eyes. A familiar feeling crept over her. She'd experienced it many times when David had lost his temper with her, but she'd never expected to get it from Luke.

'You know Heather gets out of school at three-thirty! You'd better have a bloody good reason for leaving her standing in the playground with her teacher, while you were out messing around with crayons!' Luke took the pad from her, gave it a cursory look and tossed it behind him on to the sofa. It bounced and skittered across the floor.

Gaby stood rooted to the spot, although inside she felt as if she was backing away. He just ploughed on.

'The school called me at work, wanting to know why nobody was there to pick my daughter up!'

Finally her tongue unwelded itself from the top of her mouth. 'Oh, my goodness! Heather…'

She looked frantically round the room then tried to rush past him to look in the kitchen. Luke lunged forward and put a restraining hand on her shoulder. '*Now* you're worried. Why weren't you thinking like this an hour ago?'

'But…but she had netball…'

'No. She didn't!'

'But she always has netball on a Monday afternoon! It's right there—' she waved a hand towards the kitchen '—on the calendar!'

'Not this week. There was a letter to say it was cancelled because Miss Blackwell is on some training course.'

Her hand flew in front of her mouth. 'I didn't know,' she stammered through her fingers.

'It's your job to know!' Luke ran his hands through his hair and shook his head. 'What kind of nanny are you? Unbelievable!' With that, he turned and marched to the bay window.

Gaby ran to the kitchen and tugged at the sheaf of papers clipped beside the calendar. A list of the term dates, a letter about the school choir and a reminder to bring household rubbish in for recycling were all she could find.

She ran back out into the lounge and stopped a few feet away from Luke. He was ignoring her, staring out across the river. The way the muscles of his back clenched told her he was better left alone.

'Luke? Where's Heather?'

He turned round and gave her a look that made her want to shrivel.

'When the school phoned I gave them permission to let Jodi's mum take her home. It was going to take me at least half an hour to get there, and Patricia Allford had offered to give her tea, so it seemed like the least painful solution for everyone.'

Gaby's stomach quivered. 'So…you came back here to look for me?'

Luke just blinked, long and slow. She swallowed.

'There was me thinking you were lying unconscious on the bathroom floor or something. Stupid, huh?'

She closed her eyes. 'Luke, I'm sorry. I really am. I just don't know how I could have—'

'Forget it.'

The look on his face said it was anything but forgotten.

'Let me go and pick her up. I can apologise to Mrs Allford in person then.'

Luke marched out into the hall and she heard the rattling of keys. 'I'll go.' The door slammed and she flinched.

This was awful! How could she? She'd been so caught up in herself that she hadn't spared a thought for Heather. She crossed the room to where her discarded sketch book lay, and stared at it.

Luke was right. She was useless. Sure, he hadn't said as much, but she could see it in his face. That same look that David had always had when he was about to go on one of his rants. Only this time it wasn't over something as trivial as a suit left at the dry cleaners. This time she'd really screwed up.

She picked up the pad and flipped the cover to look at the drawing. Suddenly it appeared awkward and childish. She ripped the page out and threw it on the cold but waiting fire. Kindling was all it was good for. Then she fetched the matches. Two minutes later, her afternoon of joy was a plume of smoke snaking its way out of the chimney.

Luke made himself ease off the accelerator. Driving at this speed in winding country lanes was not a good idea. But if he allowed the adrenaline surge to subside, he was going to have to face thoughts he was trying to avoid. Like the fact that Gaby had made a simple mistake. It could easily have been him in her position. He only half-remembered the letter in question himself, and probably would have forgotten all about it if the school hadn't phoned.

He also didn't want to face the fact that anger had been bubbling under the surface since the beach trip. Unreasonable anger. Jealousy, if he put the proper label on it. Stuipid, childish jealousy he could do nothing to quench.

He tapped the lever for the windscreen wipers. The good weather had held on long enough and now the rain was falling thick and fast. It was too early to go and get Heather. Patricia Allford had said to pick her up at six, and it was only just five o'clock.

He drove into the village and parked his car along the front. A walk on the beach might clear his head. It would serve him right if he got drenched. Part of him welcomed the punishment.

He ran to the boot of his car, got his waterproof out of the back, and set off down the shingle beach, enjoying the cold wind on his face. Before long his hands grew icy and he stuffed them in his pockets. He hadn't worn the coat for a couple of weeks and was surprised to find the spare keys for the back door in the right hand pocket, along with a scrumpled piece of paper.

He spent five minutes or so feeling the pattern of the wrinkles as he walked. Finally, he grew curious and pulled it out to investigate. As soon as he saw the school's logo on the top of the page, he knew he was in trouble. He didn't even need to read the letter to know what it was.

He folded the paper up precisely and put it back in his pocket. He'd picked Heather up from school the Wednesday before last. It had been raining then too. She'd run out through the school gates and waved a letter under his nose.

Oh, hell!

He was feeling bad enough about letting rip at Gaby as it was, and now it turned out the whole episode was his fault alone. No wonder she hadn't remembered the letter! It had been sitting in his pocket the whole time, stuffed inside after he'd given it a quick once-over.

Gaby would be livid with him. At least, she ought to be.

He frowned.

She should have given as good as she'd got earlier on—but she hadn't. She'd just taken everything he had to hurl at her, yet again. She'd apologised and hadn't even answered back. Why *was* that?

He turned and headed back to the car. A thorough soaking was not going to atone for his behaviour this afternoon. He was going to have to do some quick thinking to stop Gaby whizzing back up the motorway to London. He'd do anything to get her to stay.

His stomach bottomed out. She'd only been with them a few weeks, but the Old Boathouse without Gaby seemed a hollow prospect. Heather would be devastated if she left. And he wasn't ready to handle his daughter without her yet. Strike that. More like he was too scared to handle Heather without her. What if he failed?

There was only one thing for it. He would have to convince her to stay. He needed her.

Luke hatched a plan on the way to collect Heather—who was surprisingly unfazed by the afternoon's turn of events. She didn't even mention how much she hated Jodi on the drive home.

Heather rushed into the house as usual, once they'd parked the car, but he took his time hanging his coat up and ridding himself of his dirty shoes. He had no idea what the atmosphere was going to be like inside.

By the time he reached the kitchen, Heather was pestering Gaby for home-made cake. But he needed a chance to talk to Gaby. Alone.

'Heather, you can't possibly be hungry already. You've only just had dinner.'

Heather gave him a *ya-think?* kind of look.

'Anyway, it's homework time.' He picked up her school bag and handed it to her. 'Finish your geography, and then we'll talk about banana cake.'

She took the bag and sloped off in the direction of her room without saying a word. Too wary of spoiling her chances of cake to answer back, he supposed.

Gaby had her back turned to him, stirring something that looked like onions in a frying pan.

'Gaby?'

'Mmm-hmm.' She kept stirring and didn't turn to face him.

'Well, I just wanted to apologise…for what I said earlier. I shouldn't have reacted like that, no matter what had happened.'

The stirring stopped. 'It's fine, Luke, really. You shouldn't be apologising to me.' The wooden spoon started moving again, slower this time. 'It was my fault. I got it wrong.'

'Well, actually…' He couldn't stand talking to the back of her head any more. Three strides and he was across the kitchen, right next to her. He took the spoon out of her hand and rested it in the pan. 'What I'm trying to say…'

Where had all his effortless charm gone? Before he'd gone away the right words would have been there, waiting for him to pluck them out of the air. Now it was an effort to string more than one or two together. At times like this he realised just how much polish had been sandblasted off him in prison. Especially when faced with a large pair of brown eyes with ridiculously long lashes.

He took a deep breath and started again. 'What I'm trying to say is that it wasn't your fault, it was mine. And I'm truly sorry I spoke to you the way I did.' He offered her the crushed letter he was holding.

Brown eyes that hadn't looked away all the time he'd been talking now fluttered to the piece of paper in his hand. She took it from him and smoothed it out.

'I found it in my coat pocket earlier. As I said, it really was my fault.'

She looked back at him. Something inside her seemed to swell, and then the shutters came down.

'It's fine,' she said, blinking once. But he knew they were empty words. There was no sense of release, no closure. She broke eye-contact, picked up the spoon and toyed with the onions some more.

He didn't move away, but watched her in silence. Then he realised he'd seen her do this before—shut herself away and gloss over something. He didn't want this. He wanted her to shout, to cry—anything but smile and tell him everything was fine.

That was what Lucy had used to do. *No, nothing's wrong, everything's fine.* And it clearly had been anything but *fine* if she had been sleeping with her boss the whole time. He hated that word with a passion now.

It would do Gaby some good to admit what she was feeling, really let rip. He stepped back and rested against the counter. What the hell did he know? Letting rip was the only way he seemed able to communicate these days, and it wasn't helping matters in the slightest.

Maybe Gaby was better off the way she was. He certainly couldn't do the warm and fuzzy stuff she did.

He finally admitted defeat and headed upstairs for a shower. Maybe she just needed time to cool off. He shouldn't expect her to snap out of it just because he was ready for her to.

When he came back downstairs, Gaby hadn't moved. The onions had been joined by tomatoes and herbs and what looked like the start of a pasta sauce was bubbling away on the stove. She was stabbing rather violently at lumps of tomato to break them up.

'That smells good. What is it?' Oh, yeah, really smooth.

'Just a basic tomato sauce I was going to add some things to. Tonight I was going to—'

Luke reached over and turned the knob on the stove to *off*. 'Tonight, Gaby, you are going to sit down at that table, put your feet up, and take a night off cooking.' He pulled out a chair and motioned for her to sit in it, which she did, a bemused look on her face.

'But the tomato sauce—'

'Will keep until tomorrow, won't it?'

She nodded.

'Great. I'm in charge of food this evening.'

She started to stand again. 'No way! I've tasted your so-called cooking, remember?'

'Trust me. You'll live.'

He opened a bottle of wine and poured a glass for her. 'First, you are going to sip this. Then you are going to have a long, hot soak in the bath while I make sure madam has finished her homework and gets ready for bed. Then we'll eat. Deal?'

Gaby took a sip of wine and looked up at him through her lashes, evidently wary of this new, polite Luke. 'Deal.'

Luke scraped the pasta sauce into a large bowl and left it to cool. He could feel Gaby watching him as he washed up the sauté pan. She must think he was ready to revert to his grumpy old self at any time.

He picked up a dish towel to dry his hands. Her teeth were biting the corner of her lip, as if she were trying to decide whether she should say something or not.

'From now on I'm not going to call you Dr Armstrong. I'm going to call you Dr Jekyll.'

Luke grinned, and then he laughed. Even Gaby gave a reluctant smile and looked away.

'I'll be back soon,' he said, and walked out of the room.

Gaby tried to turn the hot tap with her toe, but it was wedged fast. She swiped some of the bubbles away and reached forward to top up the bath with hot water.

Luke Armstrong was a surprise. It took a real man to be able to admit when he was wrong. David had raised his voice to her on a predictably regular basis, yet he had never once said sorry. How she'd ever thought he was a man worth sticking around for was a mystery to her. She shook her head and picked up a book to read while she waited for the water to go cold.

Later, as she was dressing in her comfy old tracksuit, she noticed the house was oddly quiet. She walked across to Heather's bedroom, knocked gently on the door and turned the handle.

Heather looked up from the book she was reading. 'Hi.'

'Hi there. You're being very quiet.'

'I'm allowed to stay up fifteen minutes longer if I read quietly in bed. Luke…Dad said I could.'

Gaby smiled. It was great to hear Heather call him *Dad,* even if it didn't yet fall out of her mouth naturally. She kissed Heather on the forehead. 'I'll be up later to turn out the light, okay?'

'Okay. But don't rush. This book is really good.' With that, she turned the page and carried on reading, and Gaby crept out and made her way downstairs. Luke was nowhere to be seen. She padded into the lounge, sank into one of the large comfortable sofas and tucked her legs up under herself. The fire had been lit, and the feel of its glow on her face was soporific. She hadn't even realised she'd closed her eyes until she heard the front door bang and they snapped open.

It was Luke. He stuck his head through the lounge door and smiled at her. Her stomach did a weird little bellyflop. What was that all about?

'There you are.' He walked into the room and deposited a couple of plain carrier bags on the coffee table.

'What have you got there?'

One side of his mouth drew upwards in a wry smile. 'Humble Pie.'

She smiled back at him as he unloaded the bags. From the delicious smells wafting her way, she was certain it was Chinese takeaway. He opened all the cartons and disappeared into the kitchen for plates and chopsticks, while Gaby peered in each container to see what was what.

Salt and pepper king prawns! Her absolute favourite.

Luke returned and they set about demolishing his 'pie'. She almost forgot as she sat there, legs crossed on the sofa, that he was her employer. A very stupid thing to do. But, as they talked and ate and laughed, she couldn't help seeing him as the man who was slowly becoming her friend.

Luke watched Gaby as she reached over for the last king prawn. She looked totally at home here. In fact, this old house hadn't felt like a home at all until she'd arrived. And, all he'd done was grump and bark at her. He'd been a Grade A pain in the backside. Well, from tonight, all that was going to change. It was about time he polished up his social skills, and Gaby certainly deserved to be the one who got to see them first.

So he made a real effort to be nice and charming and talkative. And all of a sudden, he wasn't trying, he was just doing it. And it all felt so natural that he couldn't believe he'd forgotten how. With Gaby it was easy.

Just look at her now, smiling as she pushed her plate away and took a sip of her wine.

'I haven't really told you how much I appreciate all you've done with Heather.'

'I haven't done anything special.'

Oh, no? Then why couldn't he duplicate it? Why was it so hard for him to connect with his daughter the way she did? He threw the carton he was scraping out back on to the coffee table.

'Do you think we're ever going to find some common ground, Heather and I?'

'Luke—' Gaby shook her head and laughed '—I can't believe you don't see it! The pair of you are so alike, you're practically carbon copies. Of course, you'll find some common ground.'

'We are? I mean, we will?'

'Yes! She's a mini version of you. A baby control freak.'

'I'm sorry. Did you say "control freak"?'

Gaby nodded. She looked as if she were trying not to laugh. 'That's why you clash so much. Neither one of you is willing to give an inch sometimes. She needs to be in charge of her destiny just as much as you do.'

He opened his mouth to contradict her, but closed it again and stared at the ceiling. 'You think?'

'You just need to ease off a bit and she'll calm down. Stop trying to do everything for her. She's not the little six-year-old you left behind any more. And you can't make up for lost time by treating her as if she were.'

'And you think this will improve things?'

'It certainly won't hurt. You've already started doing it a little. Just keep going, a step at a time.'

'How do you know all this stuff? Is this what they teach you at nanny school?'

Gaby shuffled in her seat a little. She seemed to be embarrassed. 'Let's just say that, as a child, I used to feel a lot like she did. I know what it's like to have your whole life mapped out for you. It's suffocating. Every little thing had to be just so, or it was the end of the world. I don't know how I stood it as long as I did.'

Somehow the conversation had shifted and he knew she wasn't talking about her childhood any more. It had to be the ex-husband. What an idiot.

'Earlier on…'

'I thought we weren't going to talk about earlier on, Luke.'

'Let me finish, woman. I was going to ask you about your drawing—the one you had in the pad when you came in.'

'It wasn't very good. I threw it away. I'm a bit rusty.'

'Better than me. I have problems drawing a straight line.'

'Painting is what I really like to do. I was planning to start again in my free time. The colours on the river are just so beautiful.'

Were they? He couldn't say he'd noticed that much. Too busy looking inside to notice the world around him.

'What's your favourite colour, then?' Okay, sparkling conversation was still out of reach, but she didn't seem to notice. She looked as if she were enjoying herself as much as he was.

'Green, I think. It's hard to choose. But not that garish bright green. Soft mossy greens and deep emerald greens are my favourite. What about you?'

He was mesmerised by her. When she talked about things she loved, she sparkled. How had he ever thought of her as ordinary? She was looking right at him and her eyes were positively glowing...

'Brown.' The word was out of his mouth before he had a chance to think about it.

'Brown? Your favourite colour is brown. Seriously?' She pulled a face.

'No, not brown, I mean…'

Then he looked back into her eyes. Polished chestnut, warm and dark with gold lights. At that moment he couldn't think of a colour to top it.

CHAPTER SIX

A NOISE dragged Gaby from sleep. She propped herself up on an elbow and listened. The clock showed it was some time past three.

There it was again.

Suddenly, she was very much awake. She flung back the duvet and jumped out of bed. Her movements were swift and silent as she crossed the room and eased the door open. Everything was quiet again. All she could hear was her own magnified heartbeat. She crept towards Heather's door and pushed it gently.

Heather was fast asleep, one leg out of the duvet and an arm around a toy rabbit. Poor kid. She might act tough, but underneath she was a scared little girl who hung on to security anywhere she found it.

Gaby was just pulling the door closed again when she heard a shout. The hairs on the back of her neck immediately stood to attention.

Luke! Was he ill? You could never be too careful with Chinese takeaway. All it took was one dodgy prawn.

She ran across the landing and knocked lightly on his door. There was no answer, but she could hear him groaning and moving around inside. She stayed frozen to the spot, fingertips resting on the door, not wanting to intrude, but reluctant to go back to bed without offering help.

One more loud noise from inside the master bedroom was all it took. She pressed the flat of her hand on the door and pushed. The room was pitch dark. The door swung closed behind her and it took a good few seconds before her eyes adjusted to the blackness.

'Luke?' she whispered. 'Are you all right?'

He muttered something unintelligible.

She tried again. 'Are you ill?'

This time she managed to work out a few words. '…can't get out…'

'Do you need help getting to the bathroom?' Panic began to register in her voice. 'Luke, please! Tell me what's wrong.'

She moved closer to the bed and laid a hand on his bare shoulder. Luke sat bolt upright and she jumped back, almost falling over.

His eyes were open and he was staring—not at her—but at a bare patch of wall directly in front of him.

He was still asleep.

This was a nightmare or something. She vaguely remembered Justin sleepwalking and having what her parents called 'night terrors' when he was a boy. He used to scream and shout. Sometimes he'd walk around the house and do the strangest things—like put his wellies on and then just go back to bed as if nothing had happened.

Trying to wake Luke was a bad idea. He'd probably lie down in a second and move into a deeper phase of sleep. She would just sit on the edge of the bed and watch him for five minutes, just to make sure it wasn't the prawns after all.

Her bottom had only just started to make a dent in the mattress when he moved his head in one swift turn to stare at her. She held her breath. If he'd just woken up, she was going to have a tough time explaining her presence in his bedroom—on his bed, no less—wearing nothing but an oversized T-shirt.

But she needn't have worried. He turned away again and shuffled over to the other side of the bed. She was on the verge of breathing out her relief, when she realised he was getting out. And she watched open-mouthed as he walked calmly to the door that led out on to the terrace, opened it and went outside.

Gaby shot after him. The cold air hit her like a wall, but Luke didn't even seem to notice. Thank goodness he was wearing pyjama bottoms. She hadn't been able to tell while he was in bed. She wasn't sure she could handle coaxing her naked boss back to bed. Seeing him shirtless was bad enough. It wouldn't have been quite so uncomfortable if he were awake—in fact, under other circumstances, seeing such a finely toned torso would have been a definite bonus—but while he was unaware of her existence it felt voyeuristic.

And she couldn't think *that way* about *this* man.

He stood motionless at the railing. Coming outside seemed to have soothed the dreams that had him tossing and turning a few minutes ago. But it had to be close to freezing outside; they'd both be hypothermic if they stood here much longer. She couldn't leave him. What if he wandered down the steps? The tide was in. He could drown!

The only option was to try and get him back inside. An image of her father leading Justin back to bed when he'd had one of his sleepwalking episodes floated to the surface of her memory.

Luke still hadn't moved and she walked over to him and gently took him by the hand. His fingers closed over hers, a gesture she found oddly warming, even though it was just a reflex.

She moved towards the open door, tugging him gently. He didn't budge. There was no way she was going to manage to drag him back inside. Over six foot of solid male, versus five-foot-five of slightly out of shape female wasn't a fair contest.

'Luke?' She tried to keep her voice low and steady. 'It's time to go back inside now.' Then she moved again and, amazingly, this time he let her lead him. 'That's it. We're almost there now.'

She ushered him into the room and shut the door behind them. Then, as an afterthought, she turned the key in the lock, removed it and searched for somewhere sensible to leave it. She could hear him moving around the room, pacing, and she didn't want to waste time, so she just left it on the dressing table. Luke would scratch his head when he found it there in the morning.

Now inside, Luke began to show signs of distress again. He walked over to the door and rattled the handle, obviously desperate to escape. What was she going to do? And what was going on inside his head? Was he was back in prison, feeling trapped and powerless?

He just kept working the door handle, each attempt more frantic than the last. The top half of the door was glazed and he started banging on it with the flat of his hand, muttering something about needing to find *her.* She had no idea whether it was Heather or his wife he was talking about, and she didn't have time to work it out. If he kept slamming his hand against the pane like that, it was going to shatter. And she couldn't unlock it and let him go outside to freeze or drown. Think, Gaby!

'Come on, back to bed.'

She placed her hands on his upper arms and tried to turn him round, but he just kept banging the glass and growling in frustration. The only thing she could think of was to get between him and the door. Luckily she was small enough to duck under his arms, and wedge herself into position.

The next blow from his hand hit her clean across the cheek. He stopped and she took the opportunity to grab his hands and push him back a step or two. 'Come on, Luke. Please. Just get back in the blasted bed, will you?'

But he wasn't having any of it. He tried to walk through her as if she wasn't there. She stumbled backwards, landing against the door with the handle sticking into her back. She was trying to keep calm as she talked, she really was. But now her cheek was stinging, her back was sore and Luke was seriously starting to cheese her off—asleep or not!

'Will you just do as you're flipping told?' She was just going to have to get bossy. She shoved Luke hard and it seemed to stop him in his tracks. While he wasn't trying to engineer a break-out, she grabbed him by the hand and dragged him to the edge of the bed. Then she gave him another hefty push so he sat down.

'Luke.' This was ridiculous. He probably couldn't hear her anyway. 'You're not going anywhere. Just give up.'

Even in the dark she saw his shoulders droop. His chin dropped on to his chest and he gave a great shuddering sigh. More gently now, she guided him until he was lying on his side and got him to swing his legs on to the bed.

Flushed with triumph, she stood there, grinning in the darkness. Luke Armstrong was going to get what was good for him—whether he liked it or not!

And then she heard a sound that broke her heart. This big strong man, who had been through so much, was crying. It started as just a sniff, but pretty soon the sobs were coming thick and fast.

She couldn't stand it any more. Just couldn't bear to hear him take one more gulp. It twisted inside her like a knife. So she clambered on to the bed beside him and put her arms around him. Tears were streaming over her lashes too.

'Please, Luke. Please don't cry. I'm so sorry. I'm so sorry.'

It didn't matter that she had nothing to apologise for, that none of what had happened was her fault. It just seemed right that somebody should say it, somebody should care.

She stroked his hair and rubbed his back and gradually his tears subsided. She lay there, listening to the sound of his breath as it slowed and grew more even.

She was kidding herself. For the past few weeks she'd been telling herself that she was making a difference, helping him put his life back together, but the scene this evening had made that a farce. His wounds went deeper than she could ever imagine. All her notions of being able to make a difference seemed so pathetic.

He seemed to be more deeply asleep now. She started to wriggle away, but the instant she did so, he started to mumble and fidget again. Soothing words alone didn't do the trick, so she pressed her cheek against his back and snaked an arm around his waist. Physical contact seemed to calm him.

Somewhere in his brain the sensations must register and tell him he wasn't totally alone.

She breathed in the smell of him and felt the smooth skin of his back against her face, the contours of his muscles under her fingers.

This man deserved so much more than this.

He deserved love and happiness and a daughter who idolised him. Not this battered mess of a life. Luke let out one more heart-wrenching sigh and then she felt his muscles slacken. She was pretty sure he was over the worst now, but she'd better stay put for another few minutes, just to make sure.

How arrogant she'd been to think she could fix this family. In truth, she didn't know where to start. She was way out of her depth. One thing she could do was make sure he got a good night's sleep. She'd bet he didn't get too many of those.

So she lay snuggled against him and cried for the wasted years and the horrors he must have endured. And, when she had finished, she placed one tender kiss on his back and closed her eyes.

Something was tickling her face.

She swatted it away, but it didn't do as it was told. A few seconds later a small puff of air lifted a strand of hair that lay across her cheek. Stupid David! He was always waking her up by breathing on her like this.

And then it struck her that she had been divorced for nearly a year and it wasn't David who was breathing on her. Her eyelids shot up.

Luke! She was in bed with Luke.

She fought the urge to bolt out of bed and kept completely still. She would just have to do her cringing on the inside. If he woke up and found her here, she'd never be able to face him again.

She took a calming breath—well, as calming as she could—and tried to work out which arms and legs belonged to her and which didn't. She was lying on her back and Luke was facing her, one arm draped possessively across her torso. Pale grey light was filtering through the curtains. It was only just dawn and she had a good chance of escaping unnoticed if she kept her cool.

She inched out from under his arm, holding it aloft slightly so it didn't drag across her, then placed it carefully back down on top of the duvet. Moments later her feet touched carpet. She almost smiled with relief. Almost. Luke stirred and she froze. His hand searched the empty space next to him. Thankfully, it landed on the extra pillow she'd thrown aside and grabbed that.

Gaby held her breath for a few seconds more and, when she was convinced he had settled back down, she tiptoed out of the room.

The toast had just popped out of the toaster when Gaby heard Luke enter the kitchen. She blushed. Thank goodness she was leaning over the counter and he couldn't see her face.

'Morning, Gaby.'

'Morning,' she replied, lowering her head slightly as the blush raged more fiercely.

Anyone would think this was a *different* kind of morning after!

The thing was, her brain was refusing to recognise last night for what it had been—a friend helping a friend in need. It had all seemed so simple at the time. But now her emotions were weaving themselves into complex knots. She wasn't sure what she felt. Only that she was embarrassed and aware of him in a way she hadn't been before.

Sharing a bed with someone, even if it were just for comfort, was an incredibly intimate thing. The barriers she'd erected to stop herself becoming emotionally entangled had been mown down by one nightmare.

Professional distance? Give me a break!

Worst of all, she couldn't stop thinking about the feel of his skin against hers, the warmth their bodies had generated together. It had been so nice to hold him, to have some of the human contact she had missed in the last year.

Yes, that was it. She was just starved of affection. She was just reacting as any normal person would in the situation.

And normal people got into bed with their bosses, did they? Who was she kidding?

Well, whatever had happened, she was finding it hard to see him as her boss any more. Or the poor downtrodden man she'd come to save from himself. She let out a little huff of a laugh as she buttered her toast. Luke had put his finger on it the first time they met. In some grandiose daydream she'd seen herself as his guardian angel, swooping in to rescue him, then flitting off again when the job was done.

Only she wasn't an angel. She was just a woman. And now she was having trouble forgetting Luke was just a man underneath all the labels she'd pinned on him: employer, struggling father, charity case. The realisation he possessed a Y chromosome was starting to fuzz her brain.

'Could you pop a couple of slices in for me, please?'

Gaby swung round to face him. 'Huh?' She must look completely gormless, standing there with a buttery knife aloft and her mouth hanging open.

'Toast. Could you stick some in the toaster for me?'

'Oh! Of course.' She smiled.

'What's so funny?'

'Nothing, really. It's just that you said "toast".'

He eyed her suspiciously. 'And toast is hysterically funny, because…'

She reached for two slices of bread and dropped them in the slots. 'It's stupid really. I always say I'm going to put *toast* in the toaster, but really it's *bread* that goes into the toaster. It's only toast when it pops out again. It used to drive me mad when…someone I knew…insisted on correcting me. Never mind. I told you it was silly.'

And now she was babbling.

Luke was smiling. And that made the babble reflex even worse.

'Sorry, I'm wittering on, aren't I? I don't think I slept very well and it always has this kind of effect on me.' And now look! She'd swerved on to the subject she'd been determined to avoid. Oh, nicely done, Gaby.

'Really?' Luke ran his hands over his face. 'I think I slept pretty well last night—at least much better than I usually do.'

Her eyebrows shot up.

He must have seen them, because he added, 'I have nightmares sometimes. And…other kinds of sleep disturbance.' He was saying it so matter-of-factly. As if it were nothing. 'Not unusual for ex-prisoners, I've been told. I didn't wake you up, did I?'

She was saved from answering by the toast popping up.

'Marmite or jam?' she said, reaching for the knife and contorting her face into a perky smile.

'Neither. Just butter, if that's okay.'

He stopped and looked at her for a few silent seconds. His eyes narrowed. Gaby's heart began to pound.

'What?'

'I just thought I remembered…' He looked off into space, as if he were trying to capture a fleeing memory. 'No. It's gone. Never mind.'

Gaby turned to pick the toast out of the toaster. What if he remembered something? She was pretty sure he'd been in another realm of consciousness the whole time, but she was no expert on these kinds of things.

She placed the toast very carefully on the bread board, lining the crusts up with the edges of the wood. When she turned to get the butter out the fridge, Luke was still watching her.

CHAPTER SEVEN

GABY was mixing watercolours to try and match the uncompromising blue of the sky when she heard Heather approach. She could tell who it was without looking round. Luke's footsteps always announced his arrival. They were loud and firm, only stopping when they had to negotiate obstacles, then they always picked up their former rhythm.

Outside of an adrenaline surge—when the stomping was world class—Heather was very different. She would often creep up on Gaby. Not to spy, but almost as if she were worried her presence would not be welcome. Like now. Heather hovered in the doorway that led out of her room on to the terrace.

'What's up, Heather?'

Heather came closer and looked over her shoulder. 'Hey, that's really cool. It almost looks like a real painting!'

Gaby smiled to herself. Ah, yes. Trust a child to help keep your feet on the ground.

'How come you're so good at that? Did you have lessons?'

'I took some classes a few years ago, but I've always loved painting. In fact, I wanted to be an artist when I was your age.'

'So, why aren't you an artist, then?'

'Well. Let's just say my mum and dad had other ideas.'

Heather did her trademark eye-roll. 'Parents are *so* like that!'

'Believe me, Heather, compared to my parents, your dad is an absolute gift. He really loves you. It's just that he's a bit rusty at being a dad and it's taking him time to get used to it again.'

Heather looked unconvinced.

'He's been better recently, hasn't he?'

There was a short pause, then the girl nodded.

'Well, there you go! I wanted to do painting at college, but my dad refused to let me, so I ended up—'

'Being a nanny?'

'I enjoy my work. Don't think I don't.'

And she particularly liked being here at the Old Boathouse with Luke and Heather. She liked who she was around them. It was the closest she'd ever come to being accepted for herself.

'Anyway, you didn't come out here for art appreciation, did you? What's on your mind?'

Heather visibly wilted. 'I've been invited to a party on Saturday, but I don't want to go. I think

Luke is going to make me. He says I need to social-ise more.'

That was the pot calling the kettle black, in her opinion.

'Why don't you want to go?'

Heather shrugged.

'Well, whose party is it, then?'

There was a long pause. 'Liam's.'

'What? Liam who you go all soppy about when you think no one's watching?'

Heather looked ready to bolt.

'Steady on, sweetheart! You're almost twelve. It's normal to start noticing boys at your age.'

'Really?' Heather looked so relieved that it almost made Gaby laugh, but she kept her smile under wraps.

Heather really needed a mother to confide in. Luke was no help. He'd probably flip his lid if Heather ever mentioned boys, or sex, or any of the things adolescent girls were curious about.

'Yes. But only from a distance, you understand. Now, what have you got to wear?'

Heather pulled a rather grotesque face. Now we're getting somewhere, thought Gaby. She put her brushes down and took her charge by the hand.

'Let's check out your wardrobe.'

She dragged Heather into her bedroom and flung the doors of the wardrobe wide.

'Let's see.'

She pulled out a dress and held it up. Heather looked as if she were about to cry.

'Granny bought me that. And the rest of my dresses.'

Gaby took another look at it. Crumbs! No wonder Heather looked so despondent. It was a beautiful dress for a seven-year-old, all frills at the hem and a big bow at the back, but Heather would be the laughing stock of the party if she turned up in something like that.

'What about your dad? Surely he's bought you some clothes while you've been living with him?'

Heather walked over to a chest of drawers, pulled out a collection of too-large fleeces, some jeans and a sturdy pair of boots.

Gaby nodded sagely. 'I see. Well, there's nothing for it, then.'

'I won't go to the party?' Heather said hopefully.

'No, better than that. It's an absolute necessity we have a girly shopping trip.'

Heather's smile was so wide Gaby reckoned she could have swallowed the coat hanger she was holding.

'I'll ask your dad if we can go on Saturday. Then you'll be all kitted out for the party that evening.'

'Really?'

'Sure. I'll ask him when he gets in from work later. Now, it's about time you got on with some of your homework.'

Heather practically skipped off to her desk and Gaby left quietly, closing the door behind her. She sighed and set off downstairs to see if the chicken she'd planned for Sunday dinner was properly defrosted.

Of course, rescuing Heather from a serious

wardrobe malfunction was all fine and dandy, but it meant she was going to have to have a proper conversation with Luke. For almost a week now she'd managed to avoid any real social contact by being bright and breezy and incredibly busy.

Luke wasn't due home until ten o'clock this evening. That would mean she'd have to talk to him alone. At night.

She prodded the now-defrosted chicken. 'So, it looks like we're both in trouble, kid.'

When Luke came through the door later that evening she had a plate of cold roast chicken, potatoes and salad waiting for him.

'Hungry?'

'Starving. Thanks, Gaby.'

She watched him while he set about clearing his plate. After almost a month of hearty home cooking, his appetite showed no sign of slowing and she hoped it never would. But of course, sooner or later, she would have to leave, and then who knew what the pair of them would be eating? She couldn't stand the thought of them reverting to cardboard pizzas.

When it became too uncomfortable to sit there doing nothing, she fetched a basket of laundry and piled it into the washing machine.

'Gaby, you're not a servant, you know. I don't expect you to do the washing and pick up my dirty socks.'

'I don't mind, honestly.' She grinned. 'And I

promise you this, I wouldn't go within three feet of your socks.'

He smiled back and stabbed a new potato. 'Anyone would think you were trying to get into my good books. Is there something awful you've done that you haven't told me about?'

Gaby swallowed. 'I'd like to take Heather clothes shopping at the weekend, if that's all right by you. She could do with a few new things.'

He looked up, puzzled. 'Heather has plenty of clothes.'

'Well, yes. But it's that party she's been invited to on Saturday. She doesn't want to go because she hasn't got anything fashionable to wear.'

'Fashionable,' he echoed.

'Yes. You want her to mix a bit more with the other kids, don't you? I thought I would take her in to Torquay and we could buy an outfit, maybe even get her hair trimmed.'

'And being fashionable is important to eleven-year-old girls, is it?'

'Well, the fact she's bothered about the party means she actually *wants* to try and fit in, be part of the crowd. That's a good sign, isn't it?'

'As long as you don't let Heather go out looking like one of the Spice Girls, I'm okay with it.'

'The Spice Girls split up years ago.'

'Of course they did.'

Oh, well done, Gaby! Remind him he's lost a whole chunk of his life, why don't you?

He looked down at his plate and cut the next bit of chicken. 'I'll give you some money on Friday to cover it.'

'Great.'

Now the washing was in, she turned her attention to the dry dishes left over from lunch. Cupboards crashed and tins rattled.

'Gaby?'

She started sorting cutlery into its drawer. 'Yes?'

'Are you all right?'

'Yes. Of course. Why wouldn't I be?'

'It's just that I get the distinct impression that something is going on I don't know about. And you seem to be avoiding me.'

Her poor little heart juddered with fright. *Spoon in this space. Knife in that one—crash, clatter.*

'Of course I'm not avoiding you.' Only she was. She risked a glance at him. His face was serious and his eyebrows puckered.

'And you're sure there's nothing wrong?'

'Absolutely.' She performed her best breezy smile. 'Everything's fine.'

Luke could hear the giggling all the way from his study. Gaby and Heather had obviously returned from their all-day shopping trip. Why it took so long to trim a fringe and get a pretty party dress was a mystery. But it sounded like they'd had fun.

Without him, of course.

What he wouldn't give to hear Heather laugh like

that when she was with him. He put the medical journal he'd been reading down. At least her laser vision had gone into hibernation. He should just be grateful for every little bit of progress.

He took his reading glasses off and folded the magazine closed. If there was one thing he knew about female shopping trips, it was that the male of the species was required to grunt his approval at the spoils. It was as if the whole hunter-gatherer thing had been reversed.

Extra Brownie points would be earned if he appeared to inspect each and every purchase without them having to come and drag him out of his study. He'd learned this much from Lucy. From the day they'd been married, she'd managed to spend money faster than he could earn it. He'd come to realise that it hadn't been about the things she'd bought, it had been about the buzz.

Lucy had lived for excitement. She'd been dazzling when he'd first met her. Beautiful, vivacious and always on the verge of some new adventure. He'd been amazed she'd looked twice at him. Later, when their relationship got serious, he'd assumed that her reckless, thrill-seeking personality and his more cautious nature had been the perfect complement. He'd been devastated that night at the hotel when he'd seen her check in with her boss, Alex. Obviously he hadn't been able to offer his wife enough of the thrills she sought, after all.

He stood up, sending the office chair skidding

backwards, and marched out of the room. How was it that he could still feel the sting of her betrayal when he'd forgotten how to feel the everyday stuff—like how to be a normal, rational human being?

Perhaps seeing Heather in her party dress would cheer him up.

His study was tucked away round the back of the house, down a little passageway that ran past the mud room. As he approached the hall, he could hear scuffling and squealing. Gaby entered through the doorway that led to the entrance hall and stood with her back to it.

'Could you hold on a second?'

'I beg your pardon?'

'Could you just wait here for a minute or two?'

He made a move for the door handle, but she blocked him.

'What the hell is going on?'

'Heather would like you to see the whole effect in one go, so we just need to give her a chance to go upstairs and get changed.' Heather's distinctive thump could be heard on the stairs.

'I'm upstairs now! You can let him out,' she yelled.

Gaby moved away from the door knob to allow him to pass. Unfortunately, the passage had been built in an earlier time, when the residents' space requirements were obviously meagre, and she came close enough for him to smell the perfume she must have splashed on in the department store.

The daft thing was, it made him angry. She didn't smell like Gaby any more—of soap and fresh air. She smelled like Lucy used to, drenched in expensive scent. In the days between her death and his arrest, Luke had opened all the windows in their London home. Lucy's perfume had only reminded him of how she had dabbed it on that last night she'd gone out to meet *him,* telling her husband she was off for a night out with the girls.

It had been her best perfume. The one she saved for really special occasions. The fact she'd chosen to wear that one had solidified the half-doubts and questions he'd been having for some time. It was that scent that had caused him to jump in his car and follow her.

Gaby was looking at him. He ripped the door open, walked through it and kept going across the hallway and into the lounge.

He didn't want to analyse why making comparisons between Lucy and Gaby should bother him. He just knew he wanted Gaby to be different. He didn't want to find out that the warm, caring, serene person was a front for something else.

He was so lost in stewing over the past, he almost didn't notice Gaby enter the room a few minutes later. He looked up and knew from her reaction that he wasn't wearing his happy face. Too bad. It was the best he could do now the dark memories had started circling round him.

'Presenting Miss Heather Armstrong,' Gaby announced, with a flourish of her hand.

Luke was definitely not ready for what he saw next. It could have been someone else's daughter standing in the doorway, a hopeful expression in her large eyes. Gone was his little girl, and in her place was a stranger, her hair cut in some kind of layered style that ended around her shoulders. A stranger who no longer wore a familiar scowl, but sparkled and shone.

There was no sign of the baby pink dress he'd expected. Instead he could see hot pink jeans and a glittery silver top. True, it had sleeves, not straps, and it didn't reveal any flesh, but it was far too grown up for his little Heather.

He stood up. 'My God, what on earth are you wearing?'

Heather's face fell. 'Don't you like it? Gaby helped me pick it out.'

He shot an accusing look at her partner in crime, but Gaby didn't look one bit repentant. Instead, she looked as if she were about to rip his head off.

'She looks lovely. *Doesn't she, Luke?*'

He opened his mouth to reply, but a flash of something sparkly in Heather's ear caught his eye. He marched towards his daughter and lifted her hair away from the side of her head.

'Pierced ears! At your age? Take them out right now!'

Heather's hands flew over her ears. Now she wore a more familiar expression. The one with seven kinds of hatred for him in her eyes. So why didn't that make things better?

'You always spoil everything!' she screamed, then she spun around and raced out of the room and up the stairs.

He turned his attention to Gaby, whose face was a shade of pink he'd never seen before.

'How dare you? How dare you do that to my little girl?'

Gaby's jaw clenched.

'I'm waiting. What on earth were you thinking?'

She looked at the floor. He had a feeling she was about to unleash the torrent she'd been holding back since he'd first opened his mouth. But when she looked up at him again, she merely said, 'You're right to be angry. I was wrong to let Heather get her ears pierced without your permission. I'm really sorry. We just got carried away...'

That was it? How about telling him to get a grip, that it wasn't as if she were wearing a three-inch mini-skirt and a crop top? Or that ninety per cent of the girls in Heather's class had their ears pierced. She was just going to suck up all that righteous anger and buckle under?

It was then that he realised he wanted her to fight with him. He was sick of seeing her sweep all her negative emotions under the carpet and pretend they didn't exist. The childish urge to push the issue was so strong it was practically irresistible. He wanted to see the ever-calm Gaby lose her cool. And, underneath the layers of bluff, he thought maybe she wanted it too.

'You're such a coward, Gaby!'

'I'm *what?*'

Her chin trembled, but not with the threat of tears. It was the effort of holding back her anger. The knowledge only spurred him on further.

'You heard. You think I'm being unreasonable and you're too gutless to say it.'

She'd be right, of course, if she did tell him he was being unfair. Maybe that was why he wanted to hear it from her. Perhaps it would help stop the roller-coaster his emotions were riding on at the moment. Heaven knew he was powerless to do it himself.

But that wasn't it, and he knew it. He wanted to see her skin flush and her eyes flash, just as they were doing now.

'Too gutless?'

'That's right. You're too scared to tell people what you really think, in case they don't like you any more. Well, get over it!' He knew he was pushing her too far, but he couldn't stop himself.

'You want to know what I *really* think?'

'Yes, I do.'

She faltered when he said that, as if she hadn't actually expected anyone to be interested in what she had to say. But he could see she was revving up to it, and the adrenaline surge that hit him made him feel triumphant at the prospect.

'Okay, okay. Just give me a second.' She was all jittery, hardly able to keep still. She plunged her hands into her jeans pockets, pulled them out again and smoothed down her hair. He almost laughed at the gesture. Even when she was about to yell, she couldn't help making some part of herself more presentable.

'I think…I think you're too hard on Heather!' The words fell out in a jumble. He wasn't sure whether he thought she looked surprised or relieved she'd got the sentence out.

'Too hard?'

'Yes.'

'How?'

She shoved her hands back in her pockets.

'Come on, Gaby, don't lose it now! Don't water it down and make it nice. Just let the words come out the way they want to.'

He saw fire glint in her eyes and his stomach rolled. He'd better be ready for what he was prodding her into unleashing.

'You are a control freak, Luke Armstrong! If you can't get your own way, you have a tantrum. And you wonder where Heather gets it from!' She wasn't shouting, or at least not speaking at shouting volume, but her words carried the same vehemence as if she were shrieking at the top of her lungs.

'I think you bully her. I think you push and push to make her match the idea of the perfect daughter you have in your head. But it's stifling her, Luke! Suffocating her. One day you'll open your eyes and realise you've snuffed out the wonderful spark inside her, and she'll never forgive you for it. You'll never forgive yourself, either. So if you want that for her, just keep going the way you are, but don't expect me to hang around and watch you do it!'

All the time she'd been speaking her eyes hadn't left him. She'd fixed him with an intense, burning stare and he was unable to look away. She broke eye contact and looked at the ceiling.

'You need to give her space to be herself, Luke. To love her, you need to let her be free.'

Her eyes returned to him as she spoke the last phrase. She wasn't quite so heated now and her breathing was fast and shallow. Somewhere along the line they'd stopped talking about just Heather.

Adrenaline from the row was still crashing through his system. In the silence, he could hear it inside his head, throbbing in his ears. And all he could see were those chestnut eyes, waiting for him to respond. But, instead of being shuttered, they glowed with a defiant light.

She looked incredible. Lit up from the inside. In fact, she looked so alive that the only possible response was to close the distance between them, cup her face in his hands and kiss her.

CHAPTER EIGHT

His lips met hers and she reeled with shock. One moment she'd been ready to punch his lights out, now her hands were moving from where they'd been dangling at her sides to smooth over the muscles of his shoulders. She shouldn't be hanging on to him like this! She ought to be slapping his face.

And she probably would have done, if the kiss had been different. In the split second before he'd kissed her, she'd thought it was going to be as forceful as his journey across the room, but she was wrong.

His lips were soft and tender and working a crazy kind of magic inside her. His hands moved from her face to cradle the back of her neck and run through her hair. Any self-respecting female would melt at this point—and she didn't think she was far from it. There was already a worrying tingling in the tips of her toes.

She didn't have any choice in the matter. She *had* to kiss him back. And as she did, everything seemed to spiral in slow motion. She clasped her fingers behind his neck and relaxed into the kiss.

Oh, wow!

The pins and needles that had started in her toes, now prickled behind her knees. You couldn't lose consciousness from a kiss, could you? Luke's mouth moved from her mouth to her neck and she decided it was entirely possible.

They were perfectly in tune with each other and, for once in her life, everything seemed to be a perfect fit. Being here in Luke's arms felt so natural, so right. She forgot all the reasons why this was sheer madness and lost herself in the moment.

The sound of a door banging upstairs made them spring apart like a pair of guilty fourteen-year-olds caught behind the bike sheds. They stared at each other, eyes like saucers. If it were any consolation, he looked twice as shocked as she felt.

'Heather,' she managed to croak.

His tore his eyes from her and focused on the door. 'Yes. Heather. Right. I'd better go and—'

'Yes, you'd better.'

And then he was gone. Gaby slumped into the nearest chair and put trembling fingers to her lips. They pulsed as if he were still kissing her.

Luke paused on the landing to muster his scattered emotions. Had he lost his mind? A quick look at the haggard face in the mirror at the top of the stairs told him he wasn't far off.

He'd kissed Gaby. The nanny!

Except she was more than that. Only he didn't

know what. He only knew she got inside his skin and he didn't know why. But he didn't have time to ponder that right now; he had a daughter to sort out. Her sobs were audible though her closed bedroom door.

What had he done?

He knocked lightly on the door. 'Heather?' Some unintelligible wailing was his reply. He pushed the door open gently and stepped inside. She was curled up on the bed, her back to him, hugging her cuddly rabbit.

'Heather, sweetheart? I'm so sorry.'

She lifted her head to look at him with surprise. And no wonder. Usually, after he'd yelled at her for no good reason, he just brushed it away and never talked about it again. All this time he'd never once apologised. Somehow it had seemed like it was admitting failure and weakness, and that wasn't what she needed from him. How could he have got it so wrong?

'I really am sorry, darling. Will you forgive me?'

Now she sat up and looked at him. 'Me? Forgive you?'

'Yes. Dads make mistakes sometimes too, you know. And I think I've been making far too many since we've been living together again.'

Heather sniffed and he offered her a tissue from the box on the dressing table.

'I wish I could start it all again, go back a few months and be a different kind of dad. A better one, anyway. I know it's difficult to understand, but being away…in prison… made it hard for me to be anything but angry—at everyone and everything, not just you. And I wish I hadn't, Heather.' His voice began to wobble. 'I love you so much. And I'm so sorry.'

Heather reached out and touched the place where a tear was trailing down his left cheek. She followed it with her finger, clearly astonished at the sight of it. And then her face crumpled and her own tears came hot and fast. He pulled her into his arms and she clung on to him. They stayed there, rocking almost imperceptibly, for what seemed an age.

When finally it didn't seem like an impossible task to loosen his arms, he pulled away from her and looked into her eyes. She was still confused, but the rage was no longer there.

'I meant it, sweetheart. I want to try and do things differently from now on. I can't promise I'm going to get it right all the time, but I'm going to try my hardest. You're all I've got and I don't want to lose you.'

She nodded, then smiled a little. And he knew she'd forgiven him. Just like that. All he'd needed to do was open up to her a little, show her it was hard for him too, and then they could weather the storms together.

'Stand up and show me your outfit again.'

Heather shook her head and curled forwards slightly.

'I'm sorry I shouted at you earlier. I was just surprised at how grown-up you looked. Scared I was going to lose my little girl before I got to know her again, I suppose.'

Heather didn't stand up, but she stretched out a little so he could see her top.

'It's very pretty,' he said. 'And you look beautiful in it. A lot like your mum, in fact.' That had to have been the first time he'd talked about her mother with her since his release.

'Really?'

'Sure. You're going to be the belle of the ball.'

She blushed and looked away. 'It's only a stupid party, Dad.'

He smiled and stroked her hair. 'Well, you'll be the belle of the stupid party, then.'

She giggled and smiled back at him, her eyes still wet and pink.

How had a little honesty been so hard? Why hadn't he just said all of this months ago? He didn't know, but he had a sneaking suspicion that Gaby had something to do with unlocking the things trapped inside him.

Gaby.

What the hell was he going to do about Gaby?

More to the point, what the hell was he going to do about the fact that, not only had he just had the most mind-blowing kiss of his life with her, but that he was dangerously close to running downstairs and doing it again?

He ran his hands through his hair and looked at his watch. He had to take Heather to the party in half an hour. Perhaps when he got back they could talk, although he had no idea what he was going to say.

I think I like you? I want to get to know you better?

It all sounded pretty pathetic.

Gaby closed the bedroom door behind her and leant against it. Luke had left to take Heather to the party and she'd crept upstairs from where she'd been hiding in the kitchen. Her fingers wandered to her lips again.

Before she could lose herself in yet another slow-motion replay of the kiss, she marched herself to the wardrobe and pulled her biggest suitcase down from on top of it. The she opened a drawer and started flinging things inside. What things exactly, she wasn't sure, but as long as belongings were filling up the case she was heading in the right direction.

She couldn't stay here now. Not just because Luke had kissed her, but also because she'd sunk into it with such enthusiasm. And, more than that, the deal clincher, was that she knew it wasn't just a physical thing.

Luke kissing her—and her kissing him back—had just solidified the vague feelings she'd been trying to stifle. She'd fallen into the trap she'd known was here from the beginning. She'd started to care too much.

She almost wanted to laugh at the irony of it. She'd promised herself she wouldn't get too close to her charge this time, and she'd just about succeeded. Oh, no, this time she'd *really* fouled up. This time she'd started having feelings for her boss.

Damn him for being so brave and vulnerable and in need of love! Didn't he know she couldn't resist a sob story?

Of course he didn't. How could he?

But the fact that Luke Armstrong often couldn't see what was staring him in the face made him all the more appealing. He thought he presented such a tough exterior, being all grouchy and keep-out-ish, but it was so easy to read him. So easy to see that it was all a front, and that underneath he was warm and giving and thoughtful.

She could pretend with him when he did his grumpy act, but when he did things like buying her salt and pepper prawns and letting her talk about things she loved without looking down on her, it was fatal.

She jammed a shoe into the case, whether it wanted to fit or not. He should have known! He should have known that sort of behaviour was going to make her fall in love with him.

She stopped, then picked up another shoe and wedged it slowly into a space in the corner of the case. No, she wasn't in love with Luke Armstrong. Not yet. But she was getting dangerously close.

And, although she was going to miss both him and Heather dreadfully if she left, it would hurt them more if she stayed. The last thing they needed right now was more emotional complications.

Just as she reached for one of her slippers, there was a light tap at the door.

She scrunched up her face and answered through clenched teeth. 'Yes?'

'Gaby? Can I come in?'

Rats! He was back. How was she going to face him when her cheeks were all flushed and her voice was all wobbly? He'd know!

'Erm…okay.'

She clutched the slipper to her chest as the door swung gently open. And there he was, filling the door frame, looking all serious and sorry and just plain delectable.

'Listen, Gaby, I'm not sure what to say about…' His eyes drifted from her to the case on the bed, then back to the slipper she was squeezing the life out of. 'Oh.'

Oh? That was all he had to say?

He stepped inside the room and closed the door behind him. She waited for him to carry on, but he seemed totally engrossed in studying the suitcase, the open drawers and cupboard doors—the general devastation. And finally, when it seemed he'd taken in each far-flung sock and knocked over bottle of moisturiser, he looked at her again.

'Gaby. I can see you're… Please don't leave!'

Her eyes widened. She'd never seen him like this before. He was actually talking straight from the heart: no filters, no barriers. Her own heart started to thump, even though it should have known it was totally inappropriate, and she heard a little mantra start up in the back of her head.

Tell me why. Tell me why.

He scrubbed his face with his hands. 'I know I was stupid, but…'

What? What, Luke?

God help her, she even loved it when he struggled like this. It made her want to throw her arms around him and finish his sentence with a kiss.

'…but I really think we can sort this out. Heather needs you. And I'm sorry for my behaviour, I truly am. I don't know what I was thinking. But, if you go now, I don't think Heather and I will cope. We're not ready yet. Please, Gaby! I promise it'll never happen again—just say you'll reconsider. Say you'll stay a little bit longer.'

Never happen again? Her heart slumped, even though she knew it was the right thing to do. Wanting to kiss your boss was totally unprofessional. Certainly not the way a good nanny behaved.

But it's the way a woman falling in love behaves, a little voice whispered.

She had to be strong. It was better to cut the ties now, before it all got too complicated. She would tell him so. He might not understand it, but she was doing it for him.

And then she looked at him and all her good intentions skittered away. Those gorgeous hazel eyes were looking right inside her, begging her to stay, and she couldn't help herself.

'I'll stay,' she said quietly, 'for a bit longer. I mean, it wasn't just you, Luke. I also, um, you know…' How on earth was she going to finish that sentence? She left it hanging.

Luke reached for her and she almost jumped at the jolt of electricity that shot up her arm. But, instead of taking hold of her hands, like she'd thought he was going to, he gently eased the slipper from her grip and placed it next to the other one on the bed. Then he walked towards the door.

'I meant what I said, Gaby. You won't have to worry about anything like that again.' He smiled, a wry self-mocking smile. 'You're the first woman I've had anything much to do with in over five years. Just put it down to over-active something or other, okay?'

She nodded and watched him leave.

Great! Here was she, going all fluttery and weak at the knees, and it was just the strain of celibacy taking its toll on him! For goodness' sake, the way he'd said it made it sound like it could have been anyone…

Patricia Allford or Samantha at the village shop, maybe.

Yes, well, that made her feel a whole lot better! Perhaps she should rejoice that, even with all her baggage, as her mother had put it, he'd noticed she was a female of the species at all. She wasn't quite invisible to the male sex, even if she was just about to drop off the edge of the radar.

She cleared a space in the tangle of clothes and sat on the edge of the bed.

She needed to remember that, for Luke, the passionate clinch this afternoon had been little more than a hormonal blip. Nothing more.

And the knowledge made her want to weep, because she knew that by choosing to stay she had sealed her fate. She was going to fall in love with him anyway and there was nothing she could do to stop herself.

'Hooray! We've got another two. Look, Dad! We're beating you.'

Luke smiled over to where his daughter was standing with Gaby, crabbing line in hand. He'd never seen her so animated, her fresh pink cheeks glowing in the April air. She adjusted the bait on her hook and dropped the line in the water again.

It had been Heather's idea, making this crabbing trip into a contest. Boys against girls, she'd decided. A few weeks ago that choice would have stung, but now he didn't mind a bit that she'd chosen to team up with Gaby.

Ever since the night of Liam's party, nearly a month ago, things had been different. He knew Heather loved him now, and the knowledge meant he didn't have to squeeze so tight in an effort to hold on to her. Gaby had been right, as usual. Giving Heather the space and freedom to be her own person had produced a transformation.

Look at her now, laughing and joking with Gaby as they tried to edge further ahead in the contest.

And look at Gaby, trying to appear cool when he guessed she'd much rather have a good ten feet between her and the bucket of crabs. She only got close to it for Heather's sake. But that was Gaby all over. She gave of herself freely, no matter what the cost. He had a lot to learn from her.

He pulled his crab line out of the water and deliberately shook the crab off before it was over the bucket of salty water.

'Oh, bad luck!' called Gaby and he looked up. Her eyes were glowing with approval, her hair scraped into a half-bun-half-ponytail thing that was about to give in to gravity. God, she was beautiful.

He felt the full force of the realisation like a punch in the gut. And then she smiled at him. A smile that said she knew he was losing the crab-catching race on purpose and that he was wonderful for doing so, and his stomach twisted further.

It was all starting to come naturally to him and he didn't know how he'd done it. When he'd strained and struggled and tried, he'd fallen flat on his face. It was the same as when he and Heather had planted sunflower seeds in their London garden all those years ago. Give the seed enough light and water and you didn't have to push and stress; it just grew because the conditions were right.

That was where Gaby had come in. She'd shone her warmth on them and things had started growing inside, whether he'd noticed them at first or not.

He strung a new piece of bacon on to the hook,

but his fingers were shaking so badly it fell off and dropped between the wooden slats of the pontoon.

It had been almost a month since they'd kissed and he'd expected that the urge to repeat the experience would dwindle. Not so. If anything, it was gathering momentum—so much so that sometimes he could hardly think of anything else.

But she'd been right about that too. Heather was the important thing, not his own out-of-control emotions. The kiss had been a mistake. Typical that Gaby had seen that straight away and it had taken him a while to see the wisdom of it.

When he thought of the damage he might have caused if he'd actually gone in there, as he'd planned, and suggest they see where things went…

Hopefully, a few more weeks and his body, heart—whatever you wanted to call it—would catch on too. Then the sinking feeling he got every time he remembered there could never be anything between them would go.

He was still staring in her direction and she got his attention with a little wave. 'You're overdoing it,' she mouthed behind Heather's back.

Huh?

She pointed to the crab line still dangling empty in his hands, nowhere near the water, and he realised he'd forgotten he was pretending to lose. He was losing for real.

'Thirty-seven…thirty-eight…thirty nine.'

Gaby winced as Luke picked each crab up by

the back of its shell and dropped it carefully back into the river.

'You beat me by a long way, girls.'

Girls?

The truth was, she felt sixteen all over again, so he might as well go ahead and call her a girl. She certainly wasn't acting like a grown-up. Grown women didn't harbour hopeless crushes for their bosses. The smile stayed put on her face, but the life behind it died. It was all getting too much. Pretending she didn't notice every time he walked into a room, trying not to show her heart was melting when she watched him with Heather. All too much.

She was past the point of no return now. She loved him. What was she going to do? Staying was pathetic, but leaving was just too hard. And anyway, although Luke and Heather were doing much better, it was still early days.

In a few months, when everything was more settled, she'd leave. They'd be able to find a new nanny and she'd go. She promised herself she would ring the agency in a couple of weeks and start them looking for a permanent replacement. In fact, she'd do it right now, just to prove to herself she wasn't as spineless as she thought she was.

She pulled her mobile phone out of the back pocket of her jeans, but before she could scroll down to find the Bright Sparks Agency number, she noticed a flashing icon that told her she had a voicemail message.

She hadn't heard the bleep announcing its arrival, but Heather had been squealing so much it was hardly surprising. She punched a sequence of buttons and waited to hear who the message was from.

'Gabrielle?' her mother's voice screeched in her ear. 'Just to let you know the party starts at eight o'clock and I'd like you to be there on the dot. Do wear something nice, won't you? Bye.'

Oh, yes. Next Saturday was the sixteenth. Justin's party. She'd been intending to wriggle out of it, but maybe this was just what she needed. A weekend away from Luke and the Old Boathouse might give her some time to herself. The luxury of not being constantly terrified she was going to give herself away, scared that Luke would be able to read the damped-down emotions all over her face, was very tempting.

'Anything important?'

Luke had finished releasing the crabs and was winding up the crab lines while Heather stacked the buckets together.

'Actually, I was wondering if I could have the whole of next weekend off. It's my brother's birthday party.'

'That shouldn't be a problem. You haven't taken as many days off as you could have, and I could take some annual leave and spend some time with Heather myself.'

Yes. That would be good. A few days with just the two of them was just what they needed. It would be good practice for when she left for good. She couldn't always be a buffer for them.

Heather joined them. 'Does that mean we can go and visit Granny and Grandpa like you promised?'

Luke didn't do a terribly good job of hiding his reaction to that question. 'Erm, we'll see.'

'Dad! You promised!'

'I said, "We'll see", didn't I?'

'That always means no.'

She was right. Heather was as sharp as a pin when it came to getting what she wanted. Pity she didn't apply the same lateral thinking to her homework.

'Okay. We'll go and visit your grandparents.'

'Cool! Can I have an ice cream?'

Luke found some change in his pocket and shook his head as Heather ran away with it to the newsagent's.

'Don't you get on with your parents?' Gaby asked, feeling a little nosey. Luke hardly ever talked about his life before the Old Boathouse—prison, his family, his wife—nothing.

'Oh, no, I get on fine with my parents, but they're living in Spain now. I'm planning to take Heather out for a long visit in the summer holidays.' He hesitated. 'You could come too, if you wanted.'

Gaby said nothing. She'd be gone by then.

'It's Lucy's parents we're going to visit.'

'And you don't like them?'

'It's not that. Things were fine before Lucy died…' He looked up the river, his brow creased.

'Luke, you don't have to explain to me, really you don't.' She didn't want to hear about the wonderful Lucy, the woman who'd broken his heart.

'No, it's okay.' They started to walk up the pontoons into the village. 'After I was arrested, I could see it in their faces—they weren't convinced I didn't have something to do with Lucy's death. They were angry, I suppose, and I was an easy person to be angry with at the time. I suspect now it was because they couldn't handle thinking badly of Lucy, of how she'd betrayed me and Heather. It must have been easier to ignore all of that if I was the villain of the piece.'

Gaby covered her mouth with her hand. How could anyone who knew Luke think he was capable of such a thing? 'Do they…do they still think…?'

Luke shook his head. 'No. They realised quite quickly, actually. But it changed things. They guessed I'd known what they thought, and now they can't quite look me in the eye.'

'I can understand why you wouldn't want to spend a weekend with them, then. It must be really awkward.'

'Exactly. But I'm going to tough it out anyway. For Heather. She adores them, and I really shouldn't have left it this long to pay a visit.'

She laughed. 'I'd swap with you if I could, you know. I'd much rather spend a weekend with Heather than I would go to this party.'

'Sibling rivalry?'

'No point. Justin beats me hands down in every

category. It's just that I'm going to have to get all dressed up and wear high heels.' She pulled a face and he smiled. 'And then I have to face my ex and his new fiancée…'

'Ouch.'

'Not that I mind about the new fiancée. She can have him. It's just that I'll be on my own and I can't stand the thought of all the *Poor Gaby* looks I'm going to get.'

'Double ouch.'

She nodded. 'But, if I don't go, my mother will have me hunted down and flayed alive.' Luke went to speak and her fingers flew out and pressed against his lips. 'Don't say it! Enough *ouches!*'

And them she regretted her foolish reflex and pulled her hand away. His lips had felt too warm, too soft. She stuffed her hand in her pocket and they walked up to join Heather in silence.

CHAPTER NINE

'STUPID, stupid car!'

Gaby banged her hands on the steering wheel, then did it once again, just to make her point.

'Has the heap finally had it?' Heather asked, not seeming too devastated by the news.

'This is not a heap. It's a classic car.'

Heather looked out of the window at the school kids streaming past and sighed. 'What, classic like an antique?'

Gaby was in no mood for Heather's lip. 'Give it a rest, will you, Heather?' she said, as she opened the door and went to have a look at the engine. Not that she'd know what to look for. If only she'd taken car maintenance rather than all those cooking courses.

The best bit of mechanical maintenance she could manage was to get her phone out and call the roadside assistance people. When she'd finished her call she climbed back inside the car.

'Sorry, Heather. We're going to have to wait about forty-five minutes for them to get here.'

Heather scowled. 'I'm going to miss that thing on telly I wanted to watch!'

Gaby bit back a smile. It was kind of nice to see Heather hadn't lost her laser vision completely, although she was very glad it had only the occasionally outing these days. She sank back into her seat and kept her eyes on the horizon for the tow truck. This did not look good.

Things didn't look much better when she'd heard from the garage the next morning. Seven to ten working days to get the part. The twentieth at the earliest, in other words. Too late for the party, and too late to escape Luke and his darn hazel eyes.

She put the phone down and walked into the kitchen.

'Looks like my weekend trip is off.'

Luke looked up from his newspaper.

'And if I'm not going away, you don't have to either, I suppose.'

He put down his paper and looked at her. 'Ah, if only it were that simple. Heather is not going to let me welch out so easily. She'll—what did you say your mother would do to you?'

'Flay me alive.'

'Right. She'll flay me alive if I cancel this trip.'

'Looks like I've got the house to myself this weekend, then.'

'Where did you say the party was?'

'Chislehurst.'

'That's only a few miles from Lucy's parents. Why don't you hitch a ride with us?'

'Um, I'm not sure.'

'Not sure about what? We're going to London and you need a lift. It couldn't be simpler. You don't want your mother coming after you, do you? Living without your skin is going to be tricky. I'm a doctor, I know these things.'

She smiled, despite her resolve not to.

'Well, it does seem a more pleasant prospect than lugging my case on the train.'

'Good. Well, that's decided, then.'

She had no idea why he looked so pleased with himself.

'Good,' she echoed, not entirely sure that six hours shut in a car with Luke was going to be anything but really, really bad for her nerves.

The motorway was a sea of orange cones. Gaby sighed and glanced into the back seat. Heather was plugged into her MP3 player and seemed oblivious to the delay. In fact, she seemed oblivious to almost everything.

'Perhaps we're both going to be saved by the roadworks,' Luke said, edging the car forward slightly to keep close to the van in front.

'I wish.'

Luke frowned and looked at her. Gaby didn't bother telling him to keep his eyes on the road. There didn't seem to be much point when they obviously weren't going anywhere.

'Don't you miss your family?'

'Of course I do. It's just…'

'Just?'

'I don't know. They have a way of making me feel…stupid.'

Luke's reply was so fast she couldn't doubt its sincerity. 'You're not stupid, Gaby. I don't know how anyone could think that. I end up feeling stupid around you sometimes.'

Gaby exploded in a loud snort. 'Yeah, right! The doctor thinks he's thick compared to me. I don't think so!'

Luke gave her one of his looks. One of the really grumpy ones. It was almost a relief to see it. She knew where she was with the old Luke. The softer-round-the-edges version was harder to fathom.

'Don't put yourself down like that.'

'I'm not putting myself down. It's just the truth. Justin's the clever one and I'm—'

'The beauty?'

Funnily enough, that was what her father had said to her when she was nine. He'd patted her on the head and told her not to worry. Justin might be the brains of the family, but she could be the beauty. It seemed like she'd disappointed him on both fronts in the end.

'Don't laugh at me, Luke.'

'I'm not.'

She stared straight ahead. 'You'd better catch up with that van if you want to get to London today.'

Luke whipped his head round to look at the traffic, which was now moving at a steady crawl, and fumbled with the gear stick.

He spoke without taking his eyes off the road. 'Didn't your husband ever say you were beautiful?'

Gaby was about to give a knee-jerk reply, but stopped.

Perfect. Fine. Classy. They were all words that David had used to describe her. But she'd often had the feeling he'd been evaluating her appearance—deciding whether she'd looked good enough to be presented as David Harvey's wife—rather than paying her a compliment.

So the answer to Luke's question was *no*. No one had ever looked at her, gazed deep into her eyes, the way a man entranced was supposed to, and said she was beautiful. But she wasn't going to tell him that.

Thanks to her mother, she knew how to look the part when she wanted to. It was just that, left to her own devices, she didn't want to look like a corporate wife or a suburban princess. She just wanted to look like Gaby.

Luke seemed to be concentrating on his driving, so she let the subject slide, relieved not to have to give an answer that would reveal the poverty of her life. Every woman should have at least one moment like that. A moment when she knew she was truly treasured.

The traffic started flowing more swiftly and, before she knew it, they were sailing along on the motorway towards the London suburbs. Just when she thought the conversation had been left behind with the cones, he echoed her earlier thought.

'Every woman should be told she's beautiful.'

She was getting a little irritated with Luke passing judgement on her failed marriage. It didn't matter if he was hitting the nail straight on the head—or perhaps that was why it mattered so much.

'What? You told your wife she was beautiful every day, did you?'

'Not every day, but enough.'

'Was she?'

'Was she what?'

'Beautiful.' She truly didn't know. There wasn't a photo to be found of Lucy Armstrong in the Old Boathouse.

Luke took a long time to answer. Too many painful memories, she guessed.

'Yes, I suppose so.'

'Really beautiful? Or did you just tell her because you thought you should? That seems like lying to me.' And in some small way she was relieved that David had never pushed the charade that far.

'Yes. She was very beautiful. The kind of woman all the men watch. The kind of woman who lights up a room when she walks in. That kind of beautiful.'

He sounded angry with her for asking. She didn't know what to say, but she could tell Luke was waiting for a response.

'Oh,' she said, and it just seemed to make him angrier.

'Is that what you wanted to know? Happy now?'

'Just fine, thank you.'

Luke seethed and gripped the steering wheel. He hadn't wanted to tell Gaby that Lucy had been stunning. It felt like awarding her points she hadn't deserved.

Yes, she'd been gorgeous. Yes, she'd been the sort of person others were drawn to, because she'd always seemed so full of life and fun. But true to form, it had taken him some time to realise there wasn't much beneath the surface.

Underneath the luscious exterior she'd been selfish and fickle and not beautiful at all. Not like Gaby was. Gaby's beauty started on the inside and shone its way outwards, lighting up everything about her. Her husband must have been a fool not so see it—and a jerk for making Gaby feel the way she did. If he ever met the guy, he'd be tempted to connect his fist with the other man's jaw.

They finally pulled into the car park of Hurst Manor Hotel a little after six.

'Don't shoot off, Gaby. I'll give you a hand with your case.' He turned to face his daughter. 'Heather, I'll be back in a sec.'

'What?' Heather unplugged her earphones and gave him a blank look.

'I'm just going to help Gaby with her case. Stay here, will you?'

'Sure.' She popped the little plastic discs back into her ears and started to nod her head rhythmically.

'Thanks, Luke,' Gaby said, as he walked round to the boot. 'You've no idea how much junk I need to make myself what my mother calls "presentable".'

Luke shook his head as he pulled the case from the boot. There was no point in arguing with her. She was totally blinkered on this point.

He followed her up the short flight of stairs to the hotel lobby. It was one of those places that had probably been an old manor house, with grand architecture and manicured lawns. This party looked as if it was going to be a posh affair.

Gaby collected a key from the reception desk and Luke followed her towards an ornate oak staircase. As they reached the foot of the stairs, he heard a loud female voice pierce the atmosphere.

'Donald! I told you we needed linen napkins for the buffet.' A thin young man behind the desk—probably poor Donald—nearly jumped out of his skin.

Gaby seemed to shrink slightly. Then she started to scurry up the stairs, motioning for him to hurry up.

'Gabrielle! There you are! About time, too.'

Gaby froze and turned slowly. 'Mum, lovely to see you. We got a bit held up on the motorway.'

'Well, never mind. You're here now. I do hope you're going to do something with your hair, darling.'

Luke could see Gaby was biting back a response, but she walked down the steps to give her mother a kiss on the cheek. 'Of course I am.'

It all made sense now. Gaby had become an expert

in glossing over her feelings from a very early age. Survival tactics. Mrs Michaels's gaze fell on him and he instantly felt all wrinkled and stale from the journey. Her eyebrows hitched just high enough to ask a question.

'Mum, this is Luke.'

The older woman looked him up and down, then returned to scolding her daughter. 'Well, chop chop, Gabrielle. We haven't got time to stand around and gas.' And with that, she swept off in search of the cowering Donald.

'Don't say a word,' Gaby warned him.

Luke couldn't help it. His mouth stretched into a wide smile.

'I'm warning you!'

It was no good. He could see the tell-tale quiver of her bottom lip. His smile widened even further.

'Oh, you rat!' she said, and burst out laughing. 'Come on, then. I've got to *chop chop,* didn't you hear?'

He followed her up to her room and dumped her case inside the door, without actually setting foot over the threshold. 'What time does the party start?'

She kicked off her shoes and leant against the wall. 'Eight. Wish me luck.'

'Good luck.'

It seemed the most natural thing in the world to lean forward and give her a kiss on the cheek, but he resisted it with all his strength. 'Bye, then. I'll pick you up tomorrow at two.'

'Two it is. Bye.'

He walked back down the corridor and when he turned to take the stairs he looked back. A perfectly natural thing to do. It didn't mean anything. She was still in the doorway, looking at him. He twitched his lips into a half smile and then he walked down the stairs.

Heather was wandering in the lobby.

'Heather? I thought I told you to stay put.'

Heather looked sheepish. 'I need the loo,' she whispered.

'Oh. Okay.' He scanned the doors for signs. 'Look, there it is, down that corridor. I'll meet you back here in five minutes.'

Heather scooted off and he found himself a wall to lean against while he waited. After hours in the driving seat, he didn't feel much like sitting. A tall good-looking man entered the foyer from the hotel bar. Luke tipped his head to one side.

That had to be Justin, Gaby's famous older brother. The hair was lighter, more gold in it, but the similarity around the eyes was uncanny. Warm and brown and full of life. He was just about to go and introduce himself when a couple walked though the main entrance.

'Justin! How are you, you old devil?'

Justin's smile was warm, just about. 'Good. Good. And how are you, David? I haven't seen you much since...'

'The divorce?'

Justin looked flustered. 'I suppose it must be…'

'Hattie invited us.' He nodded towards the cool blonde on his arm. 'I hope I haven't spoiled the surprise.'

'No, no. I'm surprised. That's for sure.'

David clapped Justin on the shoulder. 'Super, that's the spirit. You and I were such good chums once upon a time. It seems a shame to let a little family mishap get in the way of that.'

Luke was very pleased that Gaby's big brother didn't look too convinced. Still, he was polite enough not to say anything. David grinned and looked round the foyer. 'And what about your little sister? Is she here?'

'I'm not sure if she's arrived yet, but she's supposed to be coming. You know Mum, rallying the troops and all that.'

David's answering laugh was brash and hollow.

'Is she bringing anyone?'

Justin shrugged. 'Not sure.'

The smirk that passed between David and his partner at this point made Luke feel sick. This had to be Gaby's ex. He was just the kind of low-life pond scum he'd expected. And Gaby was going to have to put up with this kind of stuff all night. He knew in his gut that David didn't have the decency to stay well clear. He was the type who liked to gloat.

At least Justin looked uncomfortable. 'Listen, David, I've got to get on. I'll see you later, okay.'

Justin made his way up the stairs and David turned to the blonde and whispered in her ear. She sniggered. Luke suddenly found himself standing up poker-straight, back no longer in contact with the wall. His hand was balled into a fist and he knew he was just itching to use it on someone.

But, just at that moment, Heather rounded the corner. She sloped up to him while he was still staring at the slick-haired lout who used to be married to Gaby. David became aware that someone was looking at him and turned, a quizzical look on his face.

Luke glared some more, then held out a hand to his daughter. 'Come on, Heather. We've got things to do.'

Gaby took a deep breath and fixed a pair of simple diamond studs into her ears. There. Done. Decorated like the Christmas turkey.

It had been quite a while since she'd had to get dressed up in her gladrags and, since she'd lost about thirty pounds, none of her pre-divorce, classic-cut little black dresses would do. So she'd splurged.

Her dress was a dark raspberry colour and the most fantastic thing she'd ever worn. To hell with propriety and shift dresses! This one was a show-stopper. The neckline was daring, but not too indecent, and she still had enough curves left after the weight loss to give it the wow factor.

Her hips could do with being a little smaller, but in this dress it didn't seem to matter. The cut was so good that all it did was emphasise her waist as the gently flaring fabric fell to her ankles. This was the kind of dress she'd always wanted to wear when she'd been out to big business affairs with David, but she'd always felt too frumpy to pull off.

She stared at herself in the mirror. Her hair was swept up into a neat chignon, a few carefully teased tendrils escaping to frame her face.

This was for David. Not to impress him, but to say, *Ha! Stuff you! I can make it on my own.* And the fact that she looked ten times better today than she had done during their marriage was a testament to the fact she was right.

And everyone would see she was better off without him and they'd stop whispering and giving her pitying looks and just let her be.

That was why she was here, really. She wasn't looking forward to being aware of David and Superwoman out of the corner of her eye all evening, flaunting their togetherness. She didn't want to be reminded that her love life was pretty pathetic in comparison.

David would love to rub it in if he knew she'd fallen helplessly for someone she couldn't have. He was competitive about everything, even about who could recover the fastest after the divorce. The fact he'd had a head start with Cara while they had still been married wouldn't matter. He would see her on her own and he would judge.

She was just going to have to convince him otherwise—give the performance of her life. Be vivacious. Be elegant. Be charming and witty.

In other words, be somebody else.

Chop chop, Gaby. You've got an ex-husband to silence, once and for all.

She slipped her strappy high heels on and checked her watch. Seven fifty-nine.

Show time.

Luke ran a hand over his newly shaved chin. Was he making a really big mistake turning up here like this? It had all seemed such a perfect plan when he had been sitting with the in-laws, sipping tea from cups and saucers and ignoring the awkward silence. Now he wasn't so sure.

She might think he was intruding or something.

Simon, his ex-colleague and good friend, had looked flabbergasted when he'd turned up on his doorstep and begged the loan of a dinner jacket and bow tie, but he'd handed them over anyway. A true mate.

He tugged at the collar of his shirt. He'd always hated getting trussed up like this, but tonight he wasn't doing what *he* wanted. He was doing what Gaby needed. Ever since her slimy ex-husband had exchanged looks with his new woman in the hotel lobby, he'd known she needed someone to be with her tonight. A friend.

And even if he wanted to be more than just a friend, he would put that aside. She'd helped him in more ways than he could count and it was time to start repaying the debt.

Eight o'clock. He was right on the dot. Nothing more to do than walk up the stairs into the foyer and find her. And hope she didn't laugh in his face or look uncomfortable that he'd come. He took the stairs two at a time and walked into the hotel with more confidence than he felt.

The small lobby was busy already, full of guests milling around, looking for the cloakroom or greeting each other. Luke scanned the crowd, but he couldn't see Gaby anywhere. He spotted her brother at the bottom of the stairs, being hotly pursued by a tense-looking pregnant woman he presumed was his wife.

His gaze followed the staircase round and up to the landing, but there was no sign of her there either. Wait. His eye was caught by just the right shade of caramel lights in warm brown hair, but it wasn't her. The woman in question had her back to him and she held herself in a completely different way. Gaby always seemed so relaxed when she moved, but this woman stood tall and straight with an almost regal air. The motion of her hand as she smoothed her hair was too neat and precise to be Gaby.

What about the hotel bar? He checked. Still no joy.

He let out a breath that did nothing to dissipate the tension in his shoulders and wondered what to do next. How long should he wait here? Surely someone would tag him as a gatecrasher before long and he'd be out on his ear.

Once again, his eyes were drawn to the stairs. The woman he'd spotted a few moments ago was descending, one graceful hand sweeping the banister and the other lifting the skirt of her deep red dress out of the way of her feet.

His eyes followed the smooth-skinned arms upwards to her face and his heart did a double kick.

It was Gaby.

He blinked and looked again. Then his mouth dropped open.

This was his nanny as he'd never seen her before. She was wearing make-up, for a start, and not just that stuff she used to protect her lips from the blustery river air. The dark eyeshadow, or mascara, or whatever it was, made her eyes look huge and she wore a deep berry lipstick to match her dress. No sign of a half-mast hairdo here. Everything was pinned and sprayed and, well...tidy.

He wanted to call out to her but, all of a sudden, he had no idea what to say. It was as if he were looking at her for the first time, and he felt stupidly shy, almost as if he didn't know her any more.

She smiled at her brother, who'd been cornered by his wife, as she reached the bottom step, then walked over to kiss each of them on the cheek.

He couldn't get over it. She looked so poised and just plain stunning that he stood glued to the spot as she moved through the mass of people, greeting all with an even smile. Nobody would have guessed she'd been dreading this.

She was almost at the entrance of the function room before he remembered he was supposed to be following her.

He ducked and dived through the crowd, but she was always just that little bit too far away to call without attracting too much attention. Finally, she paused in the doorway to look around the room and he got his chance.

CHAPTER TEN

His tongue seemed incapable of movement. What was he doing here?

Gaby didn't need him. She was the picture of serenity and confidence. All his noble thoughts of rescuing her seeped away. But then, if he acknowledged the truth to himself, he'd have to admit that his reason for coming tonight was more than a little selfish.

He just hadn't been able to stand the thought of being away from her for almost a day. Rushing in as her knight in shining armour was just a thin excuse to be with her. Away from the Old Boathouse—away from labels like *employer* and *employee*—they could just be Luke and Gaby. Man and woman. The temptation to grab hold of that opportunity had been too great.

Gaby started to work her way through the guests. This time he didn't follow, he just watched. She paused to greet relatives and family friends as she moved through the throng of people, but he could see where she was headed. He recognised the dark, slicked-back hair of her ex-husband at the far side of the room and his fingers flexed and curled in an involuntary reaction.

She was so brave. Not many women in her position would have the guts to face down their ex in such a public place. If only he were a little closer, so he could enjoy her victory. He shuffled further into the room. Gaby stopped to chat to a crowd of men surrounding her brother. They were so tall and broad, he guessed they were rugby players. From this position he could scarcely see past them.

He stopped edging forward. Gaby only came up to his shoulder, normally. Even in heels she wouldn't be able to see past the wall of muscled men in front of her. She had no idea she was heading straight for her ex. His heart lurched in sympathy. At least David hadn't spotted her yet, either.

At that moment, one of the rugby players, who was probably recounting some hard-fought pitch battle, ducked and lunged to one side. Gaby must have got a glimpse of what was waiting for her if she carried on her path because, just for a second, she faltered. And then, almost seamlessly, she veered away from David and his new love, their backs still towards her, and headed for the little bar in the corner of the room.

It was only a slight hesitation—no one else had seen it—but it gave him courage. She needed him more than he'd thought. He made his way through the crowd and was only ten feet from her, when he saw she had company. The ex was closing in. He must have spotted her after all. But instead of the smug smile Luke had expected, he seemed a little taken aback.

David stood close behind her as she leant on the bar, and breathed her name.

'Gaby?'

She stopped trying to attract the bartender's attention and went very still. Luke could see her profile from where he stood. She took in a little breath, then arranged her face into a polite smile before she turned to face her ex-husband.

'David.'

'You look…'

She raised an eyebrow.

'…well, fantastic.'

'Thank you.' Her smile didn't change, or grow even a little. Luke knew it was a fake one, designed to throw David off the scent, so he wouldn't realise how uncomfortable she felt.

The rat leaned in to kiss her cheek. Luke had to stop himself launching forward. Every muscle in his body tensed as David's lips lingered just a little too long and he brushed his hand down the top of her bare arm.

He didn't want Gaby. That was plain from the remarks Luke had overheard in the lobby earlier that evening. But David seemed to think that Gaby still wanted him and he was using the knowledge to keep her off balance, at a disadvantage. Of course, he could be attempting to have his cake and eat it too. Either way, he was a rat.

'How's Cara?' Gaby asked.

The rat's smile flicked as he pulled away from her. Luke felt a sense of triumph. Good for her. She was reminding him what was what. And David didn't like it one bit. He was a smart guy and he'd seen she wasn't about to fall into a heap at his feet.

'Fantastic as always. You know Cara.'

'Not really, David. If you remember, I didn't even know of her existence until you were packing your bags to move out. It hardly gave us time to bond, you know.'

Luke grinned. A couple of months ago, he'd have bet that Gaby would have shrunk back and said something bland in response to that remark. She seemed to be getting the hang of standing her ground these days. With him to practice on, it was hardly surprising.

David changed tack and pasted on a look of concern. 'I wanted to come and speak to you, before word got round this evening, Gaby. I think you should know that...'

Gaby looked at him as if to say, *Now what?*

David continued. 'You should know that Cara and I are expecting a baby.'

The smile slid straight off Gaby's face, but David ploughed on. 'As I said, I thought I should let you know quietly, just in case someone else dropped the bombshell.'

Slime, pure slime. He wasn't protecting Gaby; he was rubbing it in.

'But…but you always said you didn't want children.'

David shrugged. 'What can I say, Gabs? People change. Perhaps it's got something to do with meeting the right person.' He rubbed her arm again. Patronising jerk! 'You'll find someone one day, just you see.'

The look of pure hopelessness on Gaby's face tore at Luke's heart.

David looked around the room. His smile said he already knew the answer to his question. 'Are you here with anyone, Gabs?'

Gaby began to shake her head and Luke knew this was his moment. He closed the distance between them and curled a protective arm round Gaby's waist.

'Yes, she is.'

If the situation had been any different, Luke would have howled with laughter at the look on the other man's face. Instead he thrust his spare hand out for a handshake.

'Luke Armstrong. And you are?'

'I'm…David Harvey. I'm Gaby's—'

'Well, David. It was a pleasure to meet you, but I'm sure you understand we can't let a lady as delicious as this hide away in the corner. Come on, Gaby. It's time you let me have that dance you promised me.'

And with that, he whisked her away, leaving David with his mouth flapping.

* * *

Luke's arm around her waist was propelling her forward. He was marching so quickly that she had to trot to keep up.

'Luke? What on earth are you doing here?'

He slowed and spun her ever so gently so that, without quite working out how she'd got there, she was in his arms and they were dancing. The jazz band Hattie had raved about played a mellow number and Luke drew her close so that one of her hands lay on his chest and her head rested against his jaw.

'I thought you could do with a friend here tonight,' he whispered into her hair.

'What about Heather?'

He spun her round and her stomach went giddy. How could the man with feet of iron dance so beautifully?

'She's being spoiled rotten at Granny and Grandpa's.'

He was making his presence at her brother's party seem so reasonable. Sane even. How could he know she'd come to this blasted party to escape the barrage of feelings and sensations every time he was near? And how was she supposed to resist him when one of his hands was burning at the small of her back and the fingers of the other hand were tangled with hers? To top it off, the smell of clean shirt laced with spicy aftershave was making it really, really hard to think.

It seemed as if Luke could read her mind.

'Don't worry. Just dance,' he said and pulled her closer.

She let out a breath and sank against him. She didn't care what his reasons were for coming here. All that mattered was that, right now, everything seemed perfect. All her life she'd been chasing after perfection and it had always been out of reach.

She was reminded of the bag of flour that had sat on the top shelf of the kitchen cupboard when she'd been married to David. One time she'd practically dislocated her shoulder reaching for it. Her fingertips had even brushed the paper wrapping. But, try as she might, she hadn't been able to wiggle it forward so her cramping fingers could grab it. And then David had walked in, reached over the top of her and handed it to her. It had been so easy for him.

No, perfection wasn't for mere mortals like her. It was reserved for those more clever and more beautiful. But someone had been careless. Someone had left a little piece of perfection lying around and she'd stumbled upon it. And now she had it in her grasp, she wasn't going to let it go until the clock chimed midnight, or the fairy godmother waved her wand, or whatever it was that happened when fairy tales turned to dust.

The song drew to a close and their feet stopped moving. It was too soon. She wanted to stretch the moment to make it last a little longer. Luke started to move away and she knew the magic had died.

'I think you're safe now,' he said, looking round the room.

Of course. It was all part of the show to fool David and Cara, and anyone else who might come along to gawp or take pity.

She looked up at him and her stomach bottomed out. Wow! He was wearing a really nice suit. His hair was combed and even the stubble was gone. Her fingers lifted from where they rested on his chest and reached for the smooth skin of his cheek. It was only at the last second she remembered she really ought not to, and diverted her hand to an imaginary piece of fluff on his shoulder.

'Thanks.' One corner of his mouth lifted.

Her stomach had deserted her and now her breathing was having second thoughts as well. This freshly scrubbed Luke was seriously yummy. Not that he hadn't been attractive before. It was just that, along with the stubble, all the crustiness seemed to have vanished, and she suspected she was getting a glimpse of what he must have been like before...everything.

Her fingertips made contact with the smooth skin of his face. How they'd got there after the diversionary tactics, she wasn't sure, but she couldn't stop herself. And suddenly he wasn't smiling any more, he was just looking at her and she was looking back at him, and everything had gone very, very still.

All except for the fingers still stroking his cheek. He let out a sigh, closed his eyes and leaned into the palm of her hand. And then her eyes were shut too and their faces were so close there was only one possible thing to do next…

'Gabrielle!'

Her eyes shot open and suddenly there was a clear foot between her and Luke.

'Mum! How lovely to…I didn't see you there.'

Her mother gave Luke an appraising glance. 'So I noticed.'

Luke stepped forward and offered his hand. 'Good evening, Mrs Michaels. Luke Armstrong. I believe we met earlier.'

I believe we met earlier? Who said that? Not the Luke she knew, that was for certain. Perhaps she'd been wrong. Perhaps there was still magic in the air tonight after all.

Her mother looked wary, but it would be rude not to shake hands, and if there was one thing Sylvia Michaels prided herself on, it was her manners. But both women watched in astonishment as, instead of shaking her hand, Luke raised it to his lips and kissed it gently. Was her mother blushing?

'Well, it's nice to see you again too, Mr Armstrong.'

'Please call me Luke.'

Her mother forgot entirely to do her queen bee act and gave him a really genuine smile. Gaby almost gasped out loud.

'And you must call me Sylvia.'

Luke let go of her hand and his returned to

Gaby's waist. Something that didn't go unnoticed by her mother.

'What do you do, Luke?' It was an innocent enough question on the surface. Luke had no idea he was on the slippery slope to a full KGB style interrogation.

'I'm a doctor.'

'A *doctor?* Well, that's wonderful.' The look she gave Gaby showed she was clearly both impressed and amazed at her daughter's ability to turn up with a suitable man. 'And how did you two meet? Was it—'

'Well, Sylvia, I think the band is starting up again. I'm sure you'll excuse us. We can have our chat later.'

Her mother actually smiled. 'Of course. I'll look forward to talking with you again.'

You bet she would! In a darkened room with a bare light bulb and guards at the door.

Luke had swung Gaby back into his arms and they were moving again. She looked back at her mother over Luke's shoulder. Mum gave her a knowing, don't-mess-it-up-with-this-one look, and then Luke turned her again and her mother vanished.

'So that's what they teach you at medical school these days, is it? Mind control.'

He laughed. 'It's just a game, Gaby. I was pre-warned and she was taken by surprise. We had the advantage'

'We?'

'We make a good team, don't we? I presume getting your mother off your back was on your wish-list for this evening?'

'Yes, it was, but—'

'Well, mission accomplished.'

They danced in silence for a few seconds. 'Luke? You don't have to, you know.'

A little crease appeared between his brows. 'Don't have to what?'

'You don't have to stay here and bail me out. They're my family and I ought to be able to handle them on my own.'

'Are you cross I came?'

She shook her head. 'I just don't want you to feel you have to—'

'Gaby, I'm here because I want to be here. I wanted to do something for you. You've been such a big help to me and Heather.'

Oh. It was just tit for tat, then? I help you with your family, you help with mine?

'Luke, you *pay* me to help you with Heather.'

'I know. Look, I didn't mean… You've helped me change too, Gaby, not just Heather. We're more than employer and employee, aren't we? I thought we were friends too?'

She nodded, then laid her head on his shoulder. So that was how it was. Friends—playing a game to fool the world into thinking she was all right. Well, she might as well play along. Otherwise the irony of the fact that the man who was breaking her heart was trying to mend it for her might just get to her.

She forced herself to sound brighter. 'Come on,

then. I'm thirsty. What's a girl got to do to get a drink around here?'

Luke manoeuvred them to the edge of the dance floor and they wandered over to the bar. 'What are you having?' he asked.

'Champagne, of course.' If they were going to play charades, they might as well do it in style.

'Of course.'

It was just a game, she reminded herself as they sipped their drinks. Luke was only helping her out. It was just that, for a moment there earlier on, she really had thought he was going to... Oh, never mind.

This is no time for fantasies, girl. Remember that. Now, stop slouching, smile, sparkle and pretend you're having the time of your life.

And, as the evening wore on, she realised they were doing a really good job. She and Luke danced and talked and laughed, and not once did she get anything but a look of approval as she saw their reflection in other people's eyes.

That was what she'd wanted, wasn't it? To avoid the Poor Gaby looks. Well, it had worked. Then why did the ache in her chest keep growing? Why did her smile feel as if it were contorting her face?

Because you want it for real. And that makes you Poor, Stupid Gaby.

And all of a sudden she needed to get away from him, needed some air. 'I'm just going to...powder my nose,' she said, with a smile that was far too wide.

Luke didn't smile back. 'Okay. I'll see you in a minute.'

She walked away and realised that feeling the distance between them stretch no longer made her ache, but gave her a sense of freedom. She bypassed the ladies room and slipped though a door that led on to the long terrace that flanked the rear of the hotel.

It was practically empty. The night air was chilly enough to deter most people in thin party clothes. She rested her hands on the stone balustrade and stared out over the gardens.

'What are you doing lurking about here?'

She'd know that voice anywhere. She didn't bother looking round. 'Go away, David.'

'You're looking a bit low, Gabs.' He sidled up to her.

'I'm fine,' she said, finally looking at him. 'And it's none of your business, is it? You gave up the right to stick your nose into my life the moment you slept with Cara.' Thank goodness.

'Just because we're divorced, it doesn't mean I don't still care about you.'

Pur-lease!

'I'm fine, David. I'm just tired. It was a long journey up from Devon and my shoes are killing me.'

'Is that where he's from? Devon?'

'Yes.'

'So how do you know each other?'

'What part of "none of your damn business" do you not understand, David?'

'You didn't say "damn" business.'

'Well, I'm saying it now.' She pulled herself up to her full height, ignoring the fact that she only just reached his chin. 'If it will make you go away, I'll tell you. I met him through work.'

'Work? As a nanny? I bet you don't get to meet too many eligible—' David started to laugh, then covered his mouth with his hand. 'Oh, that's too sad, Gabs!'

She narrowed her eyes and suddenly wished she had Heather's laser vision so she could evaporate him and leave Cara with a puff of smoke for a fiancé.

'Tell me it's not true! You work for him, don't you?'

'I—'

'Don't bother denying it. It's written all over your face. It's becoming a pattern, isn't it?'

She was getting really tired of this! 'What is?'

'Falling for men who are way out of your league.'

She leant back on the balustrade. Her voice was totally expressionless. 'I said, "Go away, David."'

'Whatever you say, Gabs.'

That man made her want to scream! She could practically feel the smugness emanating from him as he disappeared back inside. Well, let him go back to his pregnant fiancée! She hoped he went prematurely bald and Cara got stretch marks.

She shook her head. What was wrong with her? She wasn't normally plagued with vindictive thoughts like that. It was all to do with Luke. She wanted him so badly it was actually starting to hurt to be around him. Tonight was like a very cruel joke in that respect.

It was time to move on—move out of the Old Boathouse and find another job. She couldn't keep doing this to herself.

The sound of footsteps on the paving stones behind her made her jump, but she refused to let David have the satisfaction of seeing her rattled. 'I thought I told you to clear off,' she said, without turning round.

The footsteps stopped. 'I'm sorry, I didn't realise—'

She swung round. 'Luke! I didn't mean…'

He folded his arms in front of his chest and looked at her. 'What's up, Gaby?'

'Nothing. Just tired. I'm fine, really.'

'Crap!'

That almost made her crack a smile. She was rather relieved to have the old Luke back. 'Okay, you're right.'

'You seemed to be fine at first this evening, but for the last hour or so you've been a bit…I don't know. Is it me? Have I done something to upset you?'

'No, Luke. You've done your bit beautifully.'

'Is it anything to do with your ex? I just passed him on the way out here. Did he say something?'

She studied a spiky plant in a pot. 'No, not really.'

'Are you sure? I could go and mess him up a little for you.'

She met his gaze. 'Tempting, but no.' The twinkle in his eye was more than she could resist and she let out a reluctant chuckle that ended with a little shiver.

'You must be freezing!' He stepped forwards and gently rubbed the skin of her upper arms. In her already tense state, it was more than she could handle.

'Don't, Luke. Please?'

It was too much. On top of everything else, it was too much. She couldn't take him being caring and sweet—and touching her.

He dropped his hands and just stood there looking at her. His head was tilted slightly to one side, his hazel eyes warm and searching. And if anything the look was worse than the touching had been. She couldn't bear it, so she closed her eyes.

She heard rustling. He was taking his jacket off. And then she felt the warm satin of its lining around her shoulders and a tug on the lapels as he pulled it tight around her. It was like being surrounded with him, his warmth, his scent, his touch.

Opening her eyes was not an option. He was so close now, their bodies only inches apart, and his fingers were smoothing the lapels of the jacket across her collarbone. Any second now he'd move away and she'd be able to breathe again.

But he didn't move away, and she didn't know what to do. Her eyelids fluttered open.

To hell with breathing.

Luke was looking at her with unmasked longing in his eyes. No man had ever looked at her like that before, not even David. The way Luke was looking at her was more than just plain old physical attraction.

It was as if he could see through all the layers she'd painted on to the real woman underneath. And, much to her surprise, he liked what he saw.

When he tugged the front of the jacket to pull her just that little bit closer, her breathing kick-started again. Then he bent his head and brushed his lips softly across hers.

This was what she'd been waiting for. All these weeks since they'd had that screaming row, and now it was happening she couldn't hold back any longer. Her upper arms were still pinned against her sides by his jacket, but she managed to free them enough to circle her arms round his waist and pull herself to him.

And then she kissed him back, pouring all the love and longing she'd been bottling up into every second of it. This was Luke, her Luke. And she wasn't going to waste one moment by being hesitant or frightened or shy. For once in her life she was going to do what she felt like doing, and to hell with the consequences.

Luke's hands moved to explore the contours of her face and every touch, every stroke seemed to be filled with the same exquisite mixture of adoration and craving that was torturing her. Finally, he pulled away, his hands still cradling her face.

She looked up at him in wide-eyed wonder as the tiniest of smiles flickered on his lips.

'I've been wanting to do that all night.'

'Really? All night?' Her voice was barely registering.

His smile grew. 'Oh, yes.'

'I thought you said it was just pretend.'

The smile dimmed. 'I never said that. Why would you think I was just playing with you, Gaby?'

'It was supposed to be a game, wasn't it?'

He shook his head. 'Back in there, I thought we were giving them what they wanted to see—what *you* wanted them to see—but out here it's just us. No more pretending. I just can't do it any more.'

Me neither, she wanted to shout, but the words were lodged in her throat.

'This one definitely isn't pretend,' he said, planting the sweetest, softest kiss on her lips. 'Nor this one.' The next was on her jaw. 'Or this one.' Now his lips were on her neck. Oh, yes, it was all feeling pretty real to her, no doubt about it.

'For heaven's sake!'

They froze. She could hear her mother's sling-backs clopping on the flagstones.

'The woman must have some kind of radar,' Luke muttered in her ear, still hugging her close to him as they turned to face her mother.

'Is it true?' She was nearly upon them now and she was definitely in a stew about something.

'Is what true, Mum?'

'That…that…man…is your boss?'

Gaby swallowed. 'I don't see it's any of your business—'

'My daughter is cavorting around with a married man and you think it's none of my business?'

Gaby's teeth began to squeeze together as she

held back her anger. 'Mum, how dare you? I don't know who's been...'

Oh, yes, she did. David, that was who.

'Sylvia—'

One look from her mother told them that, without a shadow of a doubt, Luke had been demoted to using *Mrs Michaels* again.

'My wife is dead.' At least her mother had the decency to drop her jaw at Luke's announcement. 'And has been for more than five years.'

'Well, how was I supposed to know that? For all I knew, Gaby was working for a normal family—'

'Mum! I don't know how you can be so rude. Just because Luke's wife died, it doesn't mean he hasn't got a normal...' She was so cross she could hardly see straight. 'You know what, Mum? At this very moment, I'm thinking Luke's family is a hell of a lot more normal than mine is.'

'Well, I'm sorry you feel that way, Gabrielle.'

Gaby pulled away from Luke slightly, unable to stay still any longer, but he gripped on to her waist and wouldn't let her go. 'How do you expect me to feel, Mum? You accuse me of having an affair, when you know nothing about it. In fact, I'd say you don't know anything about me either, if you think I'm capable of such a thing.'

'Well, of course I didn't...'

'Yes, you did! Otherwise you wouldn't have marched out here, all guns blazing. I think you owe Luke an apology.'

Her mother blinked and Gaby watched her shoulder muscles tighten. Then she swallowed and took a deep breath. 'I'm sorry if I may have given the impression that I thought you were up to no good, Mr Armstrong.'

Luke gave one small nod of his head. Gaby guessed that was all he could manage without losing it completely.

Then her mother turned back to face her and she knew the apology had a sting in its tail. 'But, to be honest, Gabrielle, the fact you are...' she made a gesture with her hand '...with your employer is hardly proper conduct.'

That was it. Thirty-one years of never answering back came rushing to the surface at once. She was fed up with it. No more. Suddenly it didn't matter what her parents thought, or what David thought, or even what Luke thought.

She'd spent her whole life covering up how she really felt to please other people and it hadn't given her a moment's real happiness. Only the fake kind, where she was always terrified something would come along to capsize it if she didn't do or say exactly the right thing.

To hell with the lot of it.

From this moment on she was going to tell the truth. It couldn't make things any worse than they were now.

She gave her mother a tight smile.

'Too bad if you don't like it, Mum. It's none of

your business what I do. You can keep your opinions to yourself. If I want to, I will stand out here and kiss Luke. If I really want to, I will drag him upstairs and have my wicked way with him.' The look on her mother's face this very second was worth every bit of self-recrimination she might have tomorrow at this outburst.

Suddenly, she felt amazing, she felt triumphant, she felt…free. It was fantastic.

And since she was on a roll, she might as well finish with a bang.

'No one is going to stop me from being with the man I—'

Her mother's eyebrows shot up. Luke's hand gripped her waist even tighter.

'With the man you…?' he asked, his voice hoarse.

She turned to face him and looked him straight in the eye. No pretending, they'd said. It was too late to go back now. Her voice broke slightly as she spoke.

'With the man I love.'

CHAPTER ELEVEN

FOR once her mother WAS speechless. Not that Gaby noticed. She was too busy staring at Luke and the goofy smile lighting up his face. Up until a few seconds ago, she'd have sworn that Luke Armstrong didn't 'do' goofy smiles. Ever.

He even kept smiling as he kissed her again. She could feel his lips curling at the edges, as if he just couldn't help himself. That had to be a good sign, surely? The kiss itself was definitely a good sign. It was slow and soft and sweet, and seemed to echo everything she was feeling.

Did he really feel the same way? Or was she reaching for the moon, only to fall flat on her face once again?

But then, if Luke had been horrified by her announcement, he'd have been running through the hotel gardens and jumping over bushes to get away by now.

He pulled away to look at her and it was only then that she was aware that, at some point in the last few minutes, her mother had clopped away again. She searched his face for any hint of the urge to run. He placed a tiny kiss, so delicate it was almost just a breath of air, on the tip of her nose.

'You know I do too, don't you?'

Her eyes widened and she nodded. Her brain might be short-circuiting on the idea that a man like him could love her, but she knew one thing: Luke Armstrong was not a liar. If he said he did, then he did. Only he hadn't quite said it, had he?

She flicked the thought aside and let him pull her into the circle of his arms, her head against his shoulder. And they stood there, holding on to each other, as if they both were afraid to let go, not saying a word.

Luke wasn't sure how many minutes had passed when he realised Gaby was shaking. Not big shivers, just a constant quivering. Whether it was the shock, or the cold, or the after-effects of an adrenaline surge, he didn't know.

'You're cold.'

'Don't let go,' she whispered, holding him even tighter.

He laughed softly in her ear. 'I don't think I can.' And, even if he could, he didn't think he'd ever want to.

And then she kissed him, tentative at first, but it wasn't long before he was the one who was quivering. He'd dreamed of this, holding her in his arms, taking time to explore every inch of her face with his lips, brushing his hands down her back to feel the curve of her waist and the swell of her bottom. Reality was ten times better than the fantasy.

The chemistry between him and Lucy had been good, but after a few years of marriage he'd realised that was all it had been. Youthful hormones were not the foundation for a lasting marriage, or, if they could be, you had to build on them with something of more substance.

But it was more than neurons and pheromones with Gaby. He wanted to touch Gaby, feel her skin, breathe in her scent, not because of some growing need in his body—although the need was certainly there—but because he was speaking to her each time his fingers traced, each place his mouth caressed.

I love you.

And it wasn't just her body he was captivated with. It was her mind, her heart, her strength, her very essence. Touching was just the way of expressing his love without words. Because what he felt went beyond words, and the realisation of it rocked him. It was almost too intense to bear.

Gaby sighed and rested her forehead against his. 'Luke, we can't stay out here all night canoodling like teenagers.'

He could hear the chuckle in his own voice as he answered her. 'Are you suggesting you have your wicked way with me, after all? I thought that was just to shock the socks off your mother.'

She held her breath. Did that mean she had taken him seriously? All of a sudden, it seemed an awfully big thing to rush into. He wanted to know Gaby was ready, that it wasn't just a knee-jerk reaction to everything that had gone on tonight. The last thing he wanted it to be was the ultimate rude gesture to Dear Old Mum.

As the silence stretched, he knew she was thinking the same thing. And then he felt her put the shutters down.

'Don't do that, Gaby.'

Her breath was still warm on his neck, but somehow all the glorious feelings of a moment ago were twisting themselves into an ugly knot in his stomach.

'What?'

I don't know…that thing you do, like you're distancing yourself.'

'I'm right here. I haven't moved a muscle.'

'You know what I mean.'

He knew she did. She knew that, mentally at least, she'd been backing away.

'I was joking, you know. We don't have to be wicked at all. We can be as angelic as you like.' He'd spent five years in hell; he could wait a little longer for heaven. 'Scrambling into bed with each other, delightful as it would be, is not the way to start what might be a complicated relationship.'

'Complicated? How?' She was still on the defensive, he could hear it in the thin pitch of her voice.

'Well, there's Heather to consider, for one thing.'

She looked up at him, eyes all large and panicky.

'You think Heather won't like the idea, is that what you're saying? You think we'd better stop even before we start?'

'No, that's not what I'm saying!'

He took her face in his hands and made her look at him, just so she could see how completely serious and just plain crazy in love with her he was. 'I'm not walking away from this, Gaby. We'll make this work somehow. We'll take things slowly, do whatever we must to make sure Heather isn't unsettled by this. She loves you, you know.'

'As a nanny, sure! I'm just not sure she's going to be overjoyed that I'm in her life as Daddy's…whatever I am. See? You're right. Even that's complicated!'

'We'll just have to work something out.'

She pulled back and walked away, only a few steps, but it felt as if a great cavern had opened between them.

'Luke, you know how much I care about Heather. I couldn't do anything to upset her. She's been through too much already. If there's any chance that she'll react badly…'

'Don't say it, Gaby! We're not going to give up! There's got to be a way.'

She leaned back against the edge of the balustrade and closed her eyes. 'Well, we can't just pop up arm in arm tomorrow and make a big announcement, can we?'

'No, you're right. We can't do that. We'll just have to—'

'I'm not lying to her, Luke!'

He shook his head and marched over to stand in front of her. 'For goodness' sake, let a man finish, will you? No one said anything about lying. What kind of father do you think I am?'

Five minutes ago he'd been kissing her neck, now he felt like wringing it.

Then, to his surprise, she let out a low chuckle, walked over to him and planted a big, fat kiss on his lips. 'I can't resist it when you're grumpy,' she said, with a smile in her eye.

'Just as well.' The corners of his mouth turned up without his permission.

He took her hand and led her back along the terrace. 'What I'm suggesting is that we take things slowly, for all our sakes—yours, mine, Heather's. None of us are well equipped for things to crash and burn.'

She said nothing, but squeezed his fingers with hers.

'And, besides, we missed out on so much.'

'Such as?'

'All the dating stuff. You know, first dates, candlelit dinners, walks on the beach, that kind of thing.'

She stopped and looked at him, a cheeky smile on her face. 'Mr Armstrong, I do declare you have a romantic side lurking in there somewhere.'

He looked at the floor and scuffed a bit of grass growing between the paving stones with his foot. She tucked herself under his arm and they started walking again.

'It's okay, you know. I won't tell. You can be as

grotty as you like on the surface, I know you're soft as marshmallow underneath.'

He grunted and Gaby laughed.

'Now, there's the Luke Armstrong we all know and love.'

Her heart was pounding in the back of her throat as she waited for Luke's car to pull up the hotel drive the next afternoon. They had talked into the small hours of the night, trying to work out how best to handle the situation without freaking Heather out and had come up with some ground rules.

It was going to be complicated since they were both living in the same house, but they had decided to take the relationship one step at a time. Luke was right, neither he, Gaby, or even Heather, were ready for the fallout if they jumped into something they both later regretted.

So there was going to be no sneaking around, no lying to Heather and definitely no bedroom-swapping in the middle of the night. She thought back to the night Luke had had the bad dream and sighed.

It was such a pity, she had felt so safe and warm snuggled up next to him, but just sleeping in the same bed was never going to work. It would be like lighting a match and telling it not to burn. And then there would still be the awkward questions in the morning if Heather found out. That girl wasn't stupid.

Last night, as they'd sat in the deserted hotel bar and plotted and planned, it had all seemed real, possible even. But now, in the clear spring sunshine, Gaby was starting to wonder if it hadn't all been a dream. Something she'd wanted so much, she'd imagined it was real. She was half expecting Luke to pull up and act like he always had.

She saw the familiar shape of the Range Rover's headlights and grille emerge from the rhododendron bushes that lined the drive and her heart turned over.

This was it. The moment when she'd find out if she'd really turned back into a pumpkin after all.

Heather was waving madly, but Luke was concentrating on parking the car.

'Go on, Heather,' she heard him say through the half-open window.

'Da-ad! I'm not three any more.'

'I know that, Heather, but it's a long journey and you've drunk that can of fizzy stuff Granny gave you already.'

'Honestly!' Heather flounced from the car. 'Hi, Gaby.'

'Hi, Heather. Do you want me to show you the way?'

'Don't you start as well. I'm almost a teenager. I can find the way to the loo on my own, you know.'

'Good.' She smiled. Heather might not know it, but she was already streets ahead in the moody teenager stakes. Heaven help them when she actually turned thirteen.

She heard the creak of the car door and watched Luke get out. Their eyes met over the roof of the car.

Suddenly, she felt all shy and didn't know what to do with herself. It was as if *she* were the one who'd just turned thirteen.

She couldn't read his expression at all. He mumbled something, then circled the car to fetch her bags and loaded them in the boot. When he had finished he came and took her hand, brushing it lightly with his thumb. Even this tender gesture had her toes on fire. Only then did he look her straight in the eye.

Her heart melted. He was all messy-headed, his jaw taut and his eyes searching and all of a sudden, he reminded her of a little boy, unsure of how to act and toughing it out. She reached out and touched the stubble on his cheek. It was back with a vengeance.

He leaned towards her and kissed her lightly, his chin grazing her cheek, but she didn't mind the roughness—it was something exquisitely Luke— then he leaned in again and this time the kiss was longer. His lips dragged against hers and she laid her hand on his chest to steady herself.

'Morning, gorgeous.'

The smile he gave her made her heart skip. But she was hardly looking gorgeous this morning. She was wearing her comfiest jeans and a long-sleeved T-shirt that had been washed so many times it was fabulously soft. Pity the shape had been sacrificed to get it that way. No, he must still be looking at her through the filter of the night before, when she'd been as close to gorgeous as she was ever going to get—and even then you'd have to hail a cab to take you on the last leg of the journey.

'Morning,' she almost whispered back.

He was going for another kiss, but she stopped him with the flat of her palm.

'Heather,' she whispered.

She'd just spotted Heather's green T-shirt in the lobby before she came out into the afternoon sunshine. It gave them just enough time to put a bit more distance between them before she could see them clearly. Her blood was pounding in her veins. She felt as if she'd been caught out. The guilty feeling swelled as Heather loped towards them, eyebrows raised.

Gaby looked at Luke, who was standing ramrod straight, and almost giggled. He was trying so hard to look 'normal' it was obvious things were anything but.

'I was just opening the door for Gaby.' He pulled the door open a little too fast and Gaby got inside. Heather's eyebrows inched higher, but she skipped round to the rear door, climbed inside, jammed her earphones in and that was that.

Luke coughed, slammed Gaby's door and went round to get in the driver's side. He kept his eyes on the road ahead for a good twenty minutes before he dared glance at her. She gave him a wink and noticed him visibly relax.

Once they were on the motorway and Heather had nodded off, he became a little bolder. They talked in hushed tones—on neutral subjects, just in case. And when Heather woke up they continued in silence, both smiling as they stared at the road ahead.

Gaby breathed a sigh of relief once they were back in Devon and speeding through the country lanes. Home almost.

Then she jumped. Luke changed gear and his knuckles brushed against her thigh. Her skin was buzzing underneath her jeans. She turned to look at him, but he was staring ahead, seemingly oblivious.

Then he did it again.

She turned just her head to look at him and gave him a *you did that on purpose* look. Luke took his eyes off the road momentarily and grinned across at her. *I know,* the grin said. And Gaby wasn't sure if she wanted to kiss him or hit him. Just as well they were driving and she couldn't do either.

She looked over her shoulder at Heather, who was fiddling with her MP3 player and bobbing her head as usual. Then she relaxed back into her seat and closed her eyes.

What she didn't know was that the battery on the MP3 player had died a few minutes earlier. Once Gaby was looking in the other direction, Heather jammed it into her rucksack and turned to stare out of the window and, as she watched the fields and hedgerows whip past, she smiled like the Cheshire cat.

'Heather!'

Luke shot past Gaby and out the kitchen door so fast she hardly had time to turn round. Gut instinct made her drop the dish cloth and run after him. She followed him down the stairs to the little jetty next to the house. Heather was inside the dinghy moored there, fiddling with the rope. At the sight of Luke she froze.

'Heather! What on earth do you think you're doing?'

She looked at him as if it should be glaringly obvious. 'I wanted to go and explore the riverbank. It's a really nice day.'

'Do you not remember anything I've told you?'

Heather shrugged. Her behaviour was certainly better than it had been when Gaby had first arrived, but that didn't do anything to alter her contrary personality. No, things like this were pure Heather and nothing was going to change that.

'I don't know how many times I've told you not to go off in the dinghy—especially not on your own. Now get out.'

Heather let out a disgruntled noise, but she did as she was told, nevertheless. Gaby watched her as she climbed the steps and headed back into the house. Luke shook his head.

'Got an independent streak a mile wide, that one.'

'I'd noticed.' And she knew exactly who she got it from too. 'It's not such a bad idea though, is it?'

'What, being a little madam? Not planning to take lessons from her, are you? I don't think I could take two women like that in my life.'

She rubbed his arm. 'No, I meant about taking the

boat out and exploring the river. I could make up a picnic and we could make a day of it.'

He looked skywards and creased his forehead. 'Maybe.'

'Go on, it'll do the three of us good to get out of the house and spend some time together.'

'Okay, then. Let's do it.'

She returned to the kitchen and started hunting for a cool bag.

They'd been out on a few 'dates' since they'd been back from London. And Luke had been true to his word, they hadn't lied to Heather. The first time she'd been invited out bowling with some school friends and he had calmly told her that he and Gaby were taking the night off too and going out for something to eat. She hadn't batted an eyelid.

Step one was to get her used to the idea of them being alone together, doing social, non-nanny-and-employer things together. And she supposed the logical progression was doing things like the river trip today, spending time as a family, sort of.

They needed to be patient and lay a foundation, so that when they told Heather they wanted to be together, it wasn't too much of a shock. If a long term relationship was going to work, Heather had to be happy with the idea of her living here, not as the nanny, but as…what? Luke's wife?

She went over and picked up the tea towel she'd been holding before she'd rushed outside and scrubbed a mug so dry she almost took the glaze off.

Neither of them had mentioned marriage, but surely that was where this was leading? He hadn't actually come out and said the words, *I love you* or *Please, marry me?* but it was implied in every conversation they had that this was no fling; they were both in it for the long haul.

Getting married to Luke.

Just the thought of it made her terrified and dizzy with excitement at the same time. She only half-noticed that she'd dropped the dry mug back into the dirty washing-up water.

That night at Justin's party, she had silently prayed for one moment of perfection and it had stretched into almost a month. What if it all got stretched to breaking point, like an elastic band, and it all came pinging back to slap her in the face?

CHAPTER TWELVE

'JUST jump!'

Luke watched Gaby study the rough pebbly beach, the firm grey edge of the dinghy and the distance in between.

'I can't!'

Heather giggled behind him. The jump was only three feet or so. Who would have thought that a woman so fearless when it came to giving and loving could be afraid of a bit of water?

Of course, he could just tell her to sit down and hang on tight while he pulled both dinghy and woman on to the beach, but Plan B was going to be so much more fun.

'Heather, hang on to the painter!'

He turned to check that Heather had picked up the rope attached to the nose of the boat, then kicked off his deck shoes—no socks, thank goodness—rolled up his trouser legs and waded a few steps into the water. The ground fell away sharply and he was almost up to his knees fairly quickly.

'Do you think you can manage to jump into my arms, you daft woman?'

Gaby was trying to look mortally offended, but every bit of her was screaming *You betcha!* at him. She wobbled over to the side of the boat and grabbed him firmly round the neck. She was in his arms in a split-second, as if it were as natural as breathing to be there.

'See, that wasn't so hard, was it?' He deliberately tickled her ears with his breath as he whispered to her and he felt her shudder in his arms.

'Stop it!'

He did as he was told. They were still a step or two from the shore. 'You want me to let go? Here? Now?'

'No!' she squealed and clung on even harder. He chuckled. Plan B had definitely been the way to go.

'Okay.' He started walking again. His bare feet met the beach of flat stones, but he didn't let go, he just kept on walking.

'Luke! Heather is watching. Put me down.'

Luke looked round. 'Erm…I don't think she is.' Heather was scrambling up the rocky bank in search of the perfect place for a camp. She'd been raving about it the whole time they had been motoring up here.

'Luke?'

'Give it a rest, woman, would you? She's not watching. I'll put you down in a—' He was arrested by Gaby's insistent prodding on his shoulder.

'Luke? The boat…'

This time he did let go. And it was just as well Heather was out of earshot as he splashed back into the water to stop the dinghy drifting downstream. The river was wide here, but the currents were swift and it would have been out of reach in a few more seconds.

'Heather?' he yelled as he grabbed the rope and made back to shore with the boat. 'I thought I told you to keep hold of the painter!'

He could only just make out the red of her favourite fleece through the trees and low bushes.

'That was close!' Gaby looked concerned as he heaved the inflatable dinghy up the shore and tied it to a fallen tree at the edge of the beach.

'Sure was.'

'There's a towel in one of those other bags. Let's get your feet dry. I know the sun is out, but that water must be freezing.'

Call him a chauvinist pig, but he loved the way Gaby fussed over him sometimes. It would have taken wild horses to drag the admission out of him before now, but he actually liked giving little part of his life over to someone else, liked the way she cared about him, thought about him. He'd spent too many years being independent and lonely. It was time to relinquish control and think about being a partner with somebody, doing things together.

Partners. He'd never felt that way with Lucy. She didn't want the responsibility of sharing the decision-making with him. She'd just wend her own merry way, causing chaos sometimes, and he'd have to follow her around, patching things up and always, always holding the reins. And, in return, she'd accused him of being controlling and—what was that phrase she'd used? Oh, yes—unbearably anal.

Well, maybe he had been, but he hadn't had a choice. Somebody had to think about things like bills and mortgage payments. Even having Heather hadn't slowed her down that much. In fact, he'd secretly thought she'd resented being tied down to a baby and then a toddler. But then Heather had started school and Lucy had seemed so much happier. Of course, now he knew that had been partly due to the fact she'd not only got a part time job, but a part-time thing going with Alex, her boss, as well.

He looked across at Gaby, pulling a brightly coloured towel from one of the bags she'd packed. She looked nothing like she had at the party. Her face was free of gloop and her hair was in one of its gravity-defying topknot thingies and he thought she'd never looked more beautiful. Fresh and clean and full of life.

She glanced up. 'Stop staring into space and come over here.'

'Yes, ma'am.'

He sat on the edge of the dinghy and dried his feet.

Heather gave an almighty shriek from the river-bank. 'Dad! Gaby! I've found it!'

He slid his shoes on and followed Gaby up the bank to where Heather was standing. She'd found a little clearing in the trees where rocks poked through the scrubby grass.

'Look! It's perfect. That bit in the middle can be where we build the fire and these rocks over this side are like seats.'

She was right. Two low rocks, one longer than the other, flanked a little dip in the ground. Heather plonked herself down on the narrower rock.

'Come on, you have to try it out!'

She smiled widely as he and Gaby perched on opposite ends of the bigger rock.

'Sit on it properly, then.'

Talk about bossy! He and Gaby looked at each other and wiggled along until they were squeezed up next to each other. Heather grinned at them. It was her day and it seemed she was going to take full advantage of being in command.

Actually, Heather did quite a good job of organising Luke and Gaby into a work party to collect branches and bracken to make a little lean-to she could call her 'camp'. She insisted on eating her sandwiches inside and was only tempted out by the promise of roasting marshmallows over a little fire they built.

It was late afternoon by the time they persuaded Heather it was time to return home. The sky was getting greyer by the second and the wind was whipping the river into tiny feathery waves. They'd be lucky if they got back home before it poured down. They hurried back into the little inflatable as fast as they could and set off downstream.

Heather turned to face him, her face pink from the fresh air. 'Dad? I've had the best day!'

He grinned back, his eyes flicking first to Gaby, then resting on his daughter. 'So have I.'

Luke watched the two women in his life chatting as they sat on the central seat, hair blown in two different directions at once. They looked so happy and comfortable together it warmed his heart.

'Gaby?' Heather asked.

'Yes, sweetheart?'

'I'm cold. Can I snuggle into you?'

'Of course you can.' Gaby smiled at her, real tenderness and affection in her eyes, and lifted her arm as Heather burrowed into her side.

It was that exact moment when he knew it was all going to work out. And he knew he couldn't wait any longer. He was going to ask Gaby to marry him. Tonight, if he could work up the nerve.

There had to be a blank video somewhere in this cabinet! After all, there were hundreds of them, it seemed. And not one of them labelled. She had already tried a handful but they had films recorded off the telly on them.

She thrust her arm deep into the back of the shelf and pulled out a couple more. She sat back on the carpet, cross-legged, and jammed the next contender in the VCR. A natural history documentary. It might be Luke's; she'd better leave that one alone. She slotted it back in its cardboard sleeve and tried the next one.

It was grainy and the camera work was bad enough to make her feel slightly seasick. A home movie.

She sat back and tried to work out where it had been shot. It didn't look like the Old Boathouse and there seemed to be some kind of party going on. The camera operator lurched into a hallway and entered another room. Just lots more people she didn't recognise.

Her finger was on the eject button, but she pulled it back again. That couldn't be Heather, could it? Oh, my goodness! She looked so sweet. Hardly more than three years old, she guessed. By the looks of it, she was a little minx back then too. A woman was chasing her in an attempt to get her to go to bed. Finally she got hold of the wriggling child, picked her up and turned to face the camera.

Gaby felt all the colour drain from her face.

It was Lucy Armstrong. It had to be.

Heather had the same large eyes and long dark hair. If she took after her mother, which she most certainly did, she was going to be a knockout when she grew up. Luke was going to be beating teenage boys off with a stick! Normally she would have smiled at a thought like that, but suddenly it wasn't very funny.

She took in the resemblance between mother and daughter again. My word, it was striking. Lucy's hair was thick and sleek, a proper rich brunette. She touched the ends of her own hair. They felt ratty from the salt air and, while her own hair was brown, it was a mousey not-sure-what-colour-it-wanted-to-be shade.

When she was younger, her mother had complained she looked like a gypsy child, and suddenly she could see exactly what her mother meant. No matter what she did to it, it never stayed tidy like that.

But it wasn't just the hair that fascinated Gaby, it was the whole package. Lucy was so elegant and vibrant. The cameraman didn't bother focusing on anyone but her, and who would blame him? She sparkled. All the heads turned as she walked down the hallway, child in arms.

Something was scratching at the back of her mind, wanting to be let in. Lucy reminded her of someone, she just couldn't work out who. And then it came to her. Lucy reminded her of Cara the Superwoman. They weren't the same height or colouring, but it was something in the way they carried themselves. Whether it was supreme self-confidence or something harder to pinpoint, she wasn't sure.

By now Lucy had reached the bottom of the stairs.

'Wave to Daddy,' she said, waggling Heather's arm up and down. Her daughter was having none of it. Her bottom lip was stuck out as far as it would go. Bedtime hadn't been a favourite thing even then, it seemed.

Then she heard a low rumbling laugh she'd become so familiar with in the last few weeks. Luke had been the cameraman. Her stomach dipped again.

She was seeing Lucy through Luke's eyes.

And as she watched him follow her every movement up the stairs, she could tell what she'd thought earlier was true. He only had eyes for her, no one else.

Then the camera zoomed in at breakneck speed and only stopped when it framed Lucy's swaying bottom.

'Stop that, Luke!' she heard Lucy say. 'I know exactly what you're up to. Grow up!'

She heard Luke laugh again and then it suddenly cut to later on in the party. Gaby jumped slightly as she was jolted out of what had been a very intimate moment between husband and wife. She felt sick and jealous and shaky. And then she felt ashamed that she felt any of those things.

Luke had had a wife, she'd known that all along. It was just that he never talked about her. It was almost as if Lucy had never existed. She understood why he'd banished anything that held memories of her from his house now. It must be too painful to remember.

There was a noise behind her. She dropped the cardboard sleeve she was holding and twisted round swiftly, legs still crossed, to see what it was.

Luke was standing in the doorway, his face blank, but there was pain in his eyes.

She looked back at the screen. It was a wider shot of the party now, but Lucy was still centre screen most of the time and, even when she wasn't, you couldn't help watching her.

She looked back at Luke, her mouth slightly open, and struggled for the right words. She picked up one of the discarded tapes and held it up as evidence.

'I was looking for a tape for that film that's on tonight…'

He looked at the tape in her hand, then turned his face away as if he couldn't bear to see what was flickering on the television screen.

'Turn it off.' It was a command, plain and simple.

'I'm sorry. I didn't know what it was. I just—'

'Turn it off, Gaby.'

She put the tape she was holding down and reached for the button on the video recorder. When she turned round again, he was gone.

She ejected Lucy's tape and placed it carefully back into its sleeve. Then she tucked it away at the back of the cabinet where she had found it. Recording her film seemed unimportant now, anyway.

How long had he been standing there? She winced at the thought.

Well, she'd thought he'd erased every trace of his wife from his life and she'd been wrong. There was still a tiny part of him that couldn't let go. He hadn't been able to get rid of everything, and she could see why.

The way the camera had followed her said it all. Luke had been desperately in love with his wife, a woman who just happened to have all the style and grace of a movie star. And the dark shadow in his eyes just now told her everything she needed to know on the subject.

Luke was still in love with his dead wife.

How in heck was she ever going to compete with that?

* * *

The waitress hovered and Luke waved her away. He checked his watch. Quarter past. Gaby was late. Which was odd, because Gaby was never late.

If he believed in signs, he'd think it was a sign. Just another indication that things weren't quite what they should be. It was as if, a couple of weeks ago, there had been a subtle shift in the universe while he'd slept. The first sign was when he'd got up in the morning and gone down into the kitchen to find Gaby in a skirt. Gaby never wore skirts. He didn't even know she owned one.

Then he'd guessed she'd worn it to make an effort for him and something in the back of his brain gave him a sharp poke and told him he'd better say something to show he'd noticed. When had talking to Gaby got this hard?

In the end he'd mumbled, 'You look nice.' It was hardly going to win him any awards on the compliment front, but it was the best he could come up with at short notice. In truth, he didn't care what she wore as long as she still looked at him with that bottomless warmth in her eyes.

Gaby had looked pleased he'd noticed, anyway.

But he wondered if he should have encouraged her at all. Things were gaining momentum. Now it wasn't just skirts, it was shoes with pointy little toes and lip gloss, for goodness' sake!

The restaurant door opened and his head jerked up automatically. And then his mouth dropped open automatically too. Gaby was handing her coat to a waiter and it gave him time to clench his jaw shut before she saw him.

'Sorry I'm late! There was a backlog at the hairdressers.' She shook her hair, stopping slightly as she took in his puzzled expression, then she smiled. 'If I hadn't said anything, you probably wouldn't have noticed, would you? You men are all the same.'

Of course he'd have noticed!

Gone were the slightly messy, and very sexy, tumbling waves, replaced by shiny, straight hair with all the life ironed out of it.

'Luke?'

Gaby was staring at him and he remembered he hadn't even said hello or anything yet.

'You look nice,' he mumbled. Then he looked more closely. 'It's a different colour!'

Gaby ran a hand through her sleek hair. 'I decided to go a few shades darker. Nice, isn't it?'

He nodded, but he was lying—if you could call a head movement a lie. Where were all those lovely golden bits that lit up in the sunshine? Gone. Buried under a shade of brown that was richer and darker, yes, but fake all the same.

He didn't know what to say. All he knew was that he wanted to reach over the table and ruffle the perfect style with his hand.

'We'd better order.' He picked up his menu and stared at the words. He didn't need to look; he'd already decided what he was having while he was waiting.

He kept looking at her as they ate. Something was different, something more than hair and skirts and pointy little shoes. When she laughed, it seemed a little too loud. No more smiles that started off shyly and blossomed into a huge grin; now she smiled as if she was merely displaying her teeth for a toothpaste advert.

Gaby was pretending.

What she was pretending to be, or why she was doing it, was a complete mystery, but he knew he was right; he'd seen the signs before. And, in his experience, when the woman in your life started pretending, a whole lot of trouble was going to follow. The sinking feeling that had been creeping up on him finally turned itself round three times and settled in his chest.

His fingers strayed to the little velvet ring box in his pocket. They stroked its softness, feeling its shape, the domed top and the flat bottom, and when he'd explored every millimetre he took his empty hand out of his pocket and rested it on his napkin.

Not now. Not today.

No stars tonight. Gaby leaned on the railing of the terrace and peered at the sky. All she could see was a murky blackness, the only relief a silvery slit in the felt clouds where the moon poked through.

When they'd got back from London, after Justin's party, Luke had rapped on the little door that led from her bedroom on to the terrace. She'd opened the door, about to scold him for breaking the 'no sneaking around' rule so quickly, when he'd pushed a finger to her lips, taken hold of her hand and led her silently out on to the terrace.

She'd never seen a sky like it. So many stars that she couldn't even begin to imagine how many there were. She'd snuggled into the space under Luke's arm and just stared in wonder. They'd kissed and talked and kissed some more until the pinprick stars disappeared one by one and the sky started to turn grey.

He still hadn't said it right out to her, that three-word phrase she was longing to hear. He'd got close. She'd had a couple of *me toos* when she'd told him she loved him, and he'd said plenty of things that indicated he cared a great deal for her. She sighed. Luke was a man who found it difficult to say what he felt, she knew that. Patience was what was needed. Patience and hope.

She looked up at the sky again. Even the moon had deserted her. As she turned to make her way back to her room, she took a long hard look at Luke's door. It looked firmly shut, but it felt bolted. He'd been hidden away in his study all evening. Essential paperwork, he'd said. And then he'd gone to bed early.

She walked into her room and shut the door behind her. Luke was a night-owl. He never went to bed before midnight at the very earliest. Her alarm clock told her it was only just eleven. Something was wrong and she had a good idea she knew what it was.

Lucy's ghost was haunting them. It sounded a

little dramatic, but that was how she felt. It had started with the party video but, even though she'd tucked it away to get dusty again, the images seemed to be swirling in the atmosphere. Even though Lucy had never lived in the Old Boathouse, Gaby felt her presence everywhere.

Everything she said and did seemed to be measured against what Lucy would have done. She found herself guessing how the other woman would have laid the table, or kissed Heather goodnight, and was never sure whether she should do it the same way or go for the opposite approach.

And what was truly awful was that she knew Luke was making the same comparisons too. She saw it in his eyes, the disappointment.

She went into her *en suite* shower room and began scrubbing off her make-up with some lotion and a cotton wool pad. What did they put in this waterproof mascara? It was practically welded on! She finished one eye and stared at herself in the mirror. She looked all lopsided. And that was kind of how she felt at the moment.

But it was all going to get better. She would just have to try harder, that was all. She could be the kind of woman Luke needed. She could do vivacious and witty and elegant. Their future happiness depended on it.

David had grown bored of his mousey little do-as-she-was-told wife and she wasn't going down that road again, oh no. She wasn't going to make the same mistake twice.

CHAPTER THIRTEEN

AN HOUR and thirty-seven minutes, that was how long she'd been waiting for Luke. Technically, it was her night off tonight, although the lines between personal and professional were getting so blurry these days it was hard to tell the difference. But she'd planned an evening of pampering and relaxation.

A nice hot bath, then eyebrow plucking and a face pack. Okay, getting the tweezers out was not going to be relaxing exactly, but the results would be worth it. No pain, no gain, after all.

Luke and the pizza he'd promised Heather as a treat for tea were nowhere to be seen. Heather had got grumpier as her stomach got emptier and in the end Gaby had given up and whipped up a simple pasta supper.

The empty bowl and fork were still sitting on the table. She glanced at the clock. An hour and thirty-eight minutes.

It was not that she minded getting Heather a quick

supper, she thought as she automatically picked up the dirty dish. It was the fact that Luke hadn't rung, hadn't bothered to let her know he was running late.

She looked at her reflection in the window as she stood up from placing the pasta bowl in the dishwasher. Her eyebrows really weren't that bad. Not the finely arched brows she had in mind, but they were hardly big and bushy. She ran a finger along one. Perhaps she'd leave them after all. Luke probably wouldn't notice anyway.

She was starting to think he wouldn't notice if she had a limb removed. These days he was in his own little universe. He spent a lot of time in his study with the door closed. Catching up with the latest research, he called it. More like avoiding Gaby because you've suddenly realised she isn't the love of your life and you don't know how to tell her, she thought.

She was kidding herself, she knew. Despite all her efforts to be the best Gaby she could be for Luke, things were getting worse. He could hardly look her in the eyes these days. They both knew something was terribly wrong, but neither of them were brave enough to come out and say it.

She'd almost confronted him a couple of times, but if he said what she feared he'd say, that he'd made a mistake and they really didn't have a future after all, she'd have to leave. And, stupid as staying here when he only saw her as an also-ran to his dead wife was, it was better than never seeing him again.

She wiped away a tear that bulged from her lower

lashes. Damn! She'd promised herself she'd never be so pathetic over a man again. And here she was, cooking and cleaning and watching the clock.

Her eyes rested on the row of neatly stacked plates in the dishwasher and she gave the door a hefty shove and ground the dial round so the water started swooshing. For years now, ever since the honeymoon period of her marriage was well and truly over, she'd hated the sight of all those neat white plates sitting smartly in the dishwasher tray. It made her want to scream—which was ridiculous, they were only bits of china. But something about the whole image had reminded her of her life: ordered, functional…sterile.

And the really tragic thing was that, despite all her efforts to make her life go in a different direction, it was settling back into the same pattern. Only this time it was worse. She had never loved David the way she loved Luke. Now there was something worth screaming about.

She turned abruptly and headed for her room. It was her night off, Heather was watching TV, her homework done and checked by yours truly, despite the promise Luke had made to help her with her maths.

She was going to make the most of this time because she'd had enough. Enough of being taken for granted, enough of being left to cope and, most of all, enough of being invisible. All her life she'd felt that others only saw a ghostly version of her, never stopping to look inside to see how she might feel or ask what she might want.

Luke had been the one person she'd thought that saw her properly. The real Gaby and her heart had not been able to resist the thought, tumbling deeply in love with him. Only now, after a few short weeks, it seemed as if he had looked past the outer shell and discovered there wasn't anything underneath. Either that or he didn't like what he saw. Both options hurt like hell.

David had reached the same conclusion.

Well, she wasn't going to let Luke treat her like David had! That part of her life was over. Tonight, when Luke got back, she was going out. She didn't know where. She didn't even care. Just somewhere other than the Old Boathouse.

She applied a fresh coat of lipstick and pouted at herself in the mirror. Then she grabbed the bottle of perfume she'd picked up at the department store a few days ago and sprayed liberally. She looked down at what she was wearing. Knee-length skirt, high-heeled boots, cute little jumper. That'd do for a night out in Dartmouth. It was hardly a raging hotspot.

She was in the hall checking her purse was in her handbag when she heard Luke's key in the lock on the front door. The noise made all the hairs on her back stand on end.

Just that one noise.

All her life she'd pushed all the hurt and anger down inside herself, never daring to show it, and now it was coiled up tight inside her chest so she could hardly breathe.

She turned to face the door as it opened, her spine

lengthening into a steel rod. Luke bustled into the hall, threw his coat on a chair rather than a hook, and marched right past her.

It wasn't that he was ignoring her. He just hadn't seen her standing there. And that fact alone prompted the coil of bitter feelings to spring up like a cobra preparing to strike.

Luke reached the safety of his study and dropped into the chair behind the desk. He splayed his fingers on the polished wood in front of him. They were shaking.

It was over. More than six years since the night Lucy had been killed and it was finally over.

He'd found a voice mail message from the detective working on Lucy's case just as he'd been leaving work. It had taken more than forty minutes to get hold of him when he'd tried to ring back. He'd stayed at the surgery in the little office, sure this was a call he didn't want Heather to overhear.

They'd got him. Lucy's killer.

It had been Alex, her boss, her lover. Not her husband, as the world had once thought. He'd been ruled out in the original inquiry because he had an alibi, and with what had looked like watertight forensic evidence on the husband, nobody had delved any further. Turned out the woman who'd given him his alibi had been his *other* girlfriend.

The details were sketchy, but it seemed Lucy had discovered the other woman's existence and had flown into a rage. There'd been a fight and he'd shoved Lucy to stop her clawing his eyes out, so he'd said.

Luke grimaced. No one knew better than he how much of a hellcat Lucy could be when she lost it. The story had a ring of truth to it. He would almost have been able to feel sorry for the man if he hadn't deprived Heather of her mother. And, not only that, but he'd kept her father away from her with his lies while he'd moved to another part of the country and took up with another married woman.

It made his blood boil. It was just as well the creep would be banged up in prison where he wouldn't be able to get his hands on him and tear him limb from limb. He picked up the first thing to hand, a pencil pot, and hurled it over the other side of the room.

At the same time the door to the study flew open.

Gaby was standing there, eyes bright with fire. She'd left the ever-present mask of composure somewhere else at last. She looked so radiant he was very tempted to go and kiss her senseless, but the look on her face said he'd better not try it.

'Where the heck do you think you've been for the past two hours?'

'At the surgery. There's something I need to—'

'You know what, Luke? I don't care!'

'But I—'

'Are you not listening to me as well as not seeing me? I said I didn't care.'

He stood up and started to round the desk. She held him at bay with a raised hand.

'I'm taking the night off.'

'The night off? But—'

'You remember the concept, don't you? The one where I'm your employee, not your skivvy, and I get to do less than twenty-four hours a day?'

'Yes—'

'Good! I'm off, then.' She spun on the heels of a pair of deadly-looking boots, her hair flying outwards as she whipped her head round. He started to follow.

'But Heather—'

'Is in the lounge watching TV. She's been fed, which is just as well, unless you managed to fit a pepperoni special in your briefcase.'

He looked at the bag sitting just inside the door of his study, bewildered.

'I thought not. Bye.'

And, before he knew it, she was clomping down the hallway. He ran after her.

'Gaby! Where are you going? I think we need to talk.'

She stopped, turned and threw her head back and laughed. 'Oh, I think I'm way past talking,' she said when the sarcastic laugh ended abruptly. Her features set into a grim expression, then she started to walk away again.

'Stop!' He ran forward and reached for her wrist, easily circling it with his much bigger fingers. She went stock still.

'Take your hands off me.'

'I will. I just want you to…' He sniffed the air

around them. 'What on earth have you drenched yourself in?'

'None of your business!'

'It is when my woman is going out for a night alone smelling like…!' Like what? It was perfectly nice perfume. It was just that, after Lucy, that brand always reeked of infidelity to him.

'"My woman"? Listen to yourself, Luke! You sound like a caveman. I don't *belong* to anyone.'

'But—'

'But nothing! I'm going out and it's got nothing to do with you.'

'Like heck it hasn't!' He barged past her and blocked her exit through the back door. For a second he thought she was going to shred her way though him with those newly painted nails, but she folded her arms across her chest and glared at him.

'You said we were going to spend a night in together!' Now he sounded like a petulant school-boy.

'I changed my mind. I need a night off.'

'From what? There was nothing to do tonight except open a bottle of wine and watch that DVD you wanted to see.'

She walked up close to him. 'Now, let's see.' She counted off the reasons on her fingers. 'I need a night off being barked at. A night off being ignored while you moulder in your study. A night off from being the unpaid babysitter and general dogsbody—'

'You know I don't expect you to—'

She raised her voice and continued her list at shouting volume. 'And most of all, I need a night off from *you!*'

She pushed past him, walked down the path and got into her car, almost yanking the door off. He stayed watching through the open door as, without looking back, she revved the engine and squealed away up the lane.

Dartmouth was busy enough to be interesting, even though it was not yet in the full swing of the tourist season. Gaby chose the bar of the Royal Dart Hotel, hoping she'd avoid the younger crowds and leering singles.

She sat in an upholstered chair near the window and watched the rowing boats bob up and down in what the locals called the 'boat float', a small square of water lined with high stone walls and a little entrance tunnel where the dinghies could access the river proper. Nothing was still. The water reflected every light and bounced it around.

If she'd been looking for rest, this was the wrong place to find it. The bar was too noisy and smoky and, since she was driving, she was sitting here with her sad little lemonade watching couples greet each other and have an intimate drink before heading off to the hotel restaurant.

What was she doing here? Really?

She wasn't enjoying herself. She was miserable.

And she felt guilty. True, Luke's behaviour had left much to be desired in the last couple of weeks, but screeching at him was not the way to handle it.

So much for perfection. The perfect moment she'd wished for had been just that—a moment. Now the real Luke and Gaby were getting down to starting a relationship, it seemed they weren't as compatible as the fairy tale couple in her head. Big surprise!

But what was she going to do about it? She couldn't hide out here all night. She was going to have to go back and face him some time. And yet, she wasn't entirely sorry she'd said what she'd said, just the way she'd said it.

For years she'd been taking all kinds of rubbish from her nearest and dearest. No one seemed to think she had a brain of her own. It was as if she was made of Play-Doh. Everyone had a squish here and a squish there until she fitted the shape they thought she should be. Luke was just the last in a long line.

She took another sip of her lemonade. There had been something wonderfully liberating in her outburst this evening. Of course, she realised now she'd been shouting at the wrong man. The things she'd said were unspoken retorts to years of David's heckling, bottled up under too much pressure. It was just a pity she hadn't ever had the satisfaction of releasing them on their rightful owner. Luke might be a little difficult at times, but it was a crime to tar him with the same brush as David.

She'd better go back and apologise.

She picked up her handbag and realised she could hear a faint ringing from inside. Luke? She scrabbled to find her mobile phone amidst the pens, receipts and packets of tissues. At least, inside her handbag, life was going on as normal.

She finally tugged it free and almost forgot to answer it when she saw who it was on the caller ID.

'Mum?'

'Gabrielle.'

Gaby quickly pushed past a couple of people milling around the hotel entrance and stepped out on to the street. It was quieter out here and she'd be able to hear her mother better, although why she was phoning was a mystery. They hadn't talked since Justin's party.

Even to her own ears her voice sounded wary. 'What can I do for you, Mum?'

Her mother hesitated. This call was getting stranger and stranger. Her mother never normally wasted time when she had an opening to lecture.

'I wanted to call to see how you were.'

Ah-ha! Checking up on her.

'And to apologise.'

Gaby dropped the phone, but managed to catch it between her hand and her knee. 'I'm sorry, Mum. What was that?'

Her mother sighed. 'Justin and I had a chat the other day. He was very angry with me after his party, you know.'

No, she didn't know. She hadn't heard from Justin either. She'd just assumed she'd been branded the black sheep of the family and left to her own devices.

'I haven't talked to Justin recently.'

'Oh. Well…your big brother decided to tell me a few home truths.'

Justin? Mr Nice Guy? No way!

'I don't know what to say, Mum… Thank you, I suppose. I appreciate the apology.'

'I've never meant to hurt your feelings, Gabrielle.'

'I know, Mum.' She just couldn't help herself.

'I just want what's best for you and some-times…sometimes you seem so directionless. I didn't want you to waste your life when you have so much potential.'

Her mother thought she had potential? That was news!

'I'm a big girl now. I can make my own decisions.'

'That's what your brother said. He said I need to realise you're not like me, that you want different things out of life.'

'He's right, Mum. I do.' Only the thing she wanted most was slipping through her fingers.

'I might not agree with your choices always, dear, but I'll try hard to respect them. You'll just have to tell me to keep my nose out.'

Gaby giggled. 'Thanks, Mum. I'll bear that in mind.'

'Good. Well…just don't let that David ruin the rest of your life. You should never let a man tell you who to be.'

Or your mother, Gaby added silently. Although those days might be over, with any luck.

'That nice doctor you were with at the party seemed very keen on you.'

'I know. I'm just not sure—'

'Well, don't hang about, Gabrielle. At your age—'

'Mum!'

'Okay. Point taken. Nose out.'

Gaby felt a rush of love for her mother. It had taken guts to make this call. She knew how much Mum hated to be wrong. It was practically a phobia.

'I love you, Mum.'

Did she detect a slight sniff? 'I love you too, dear. Now, I'd better go. Your father's misplaced his reading glasses and he'll be hell to live with if he can't do his crossword.'

Luke sat in the dark, straining for the sound of Gaby's car. Heather was in bed and the house was completely silent. Except he could almost hear the echoes of Gaby's accusations whispering in the darkened corners.

She was right, of course. He was a caveman.

No good at understanding women. Boring. Too stuffy. Too controlling.

And then he realised it wasn't Gaby's shouts he could hear, but Lucy's. All those things she'd screamed at him in the final weeks of their marriage. He remembered each and every syllable. They'd stung, and he'd had plenty of thinking time in the years that had followed to mull them over.

'You're no fun any more, Luke,' she'd complained. And, if that had been true then, how much more so now? He wasn't even the same man he'd been back then. He was damaged, and they way he'd been reacting in the last few weeks—and especially tonight—just proved how much.

Gaby didn't need a man like him. She'd had to deal with enough of that kind of stuff in her first marriage. Listen to him! First marriage? As if there were going to be a second.

Of course, there might be another marriage in Gaby's future. Just not to him. He'd had the sense he was losing her for weeks now, hadn't he? Well, things had changed. He'd known from the way she'd looked at him tonight that he'd already lost her. It was just a matter of time before she handed in her notice and disappeared from his life for good.

He would miss her terribly. Not the prim and proper Gaby of recent times with her nail varnish and flat hair, but the warm and giving Gaby who had been happiest walking along the beach her hair in a mess and the most dazzling smile he'd ever seen on her blusher-free cheeks.

Perhaps it was better this way. She wasn't the woman he'd thought she was. And, if he was right about that, he would mourn the idea of Gaby rather than her living counterpart, who was doing her best to be every bit as shallow as his adoring dead wife.

Gaby dropped her bag and her hand flew to her chest. Her heart was thumping like a drum.

'Luke! You gave me a fright! What are you doing, sitting here in the dark?'

'Waiting for you.'

'Oh.'

She sat down on the edge of one of the armchairs, bottom only just making contact, knees together. She rested her hands on top of her knees and waited. Neither of them thought to switch a light on.

'I have some news.'

This is it! He's going to fire me, as both nanny and girlfriend. 'Okay.'

'I had a call from the police this afternoon.' His voice was completely emotionless. 'They've arrested someone for Lucy's murder.'

Her eyes widened and she gripped her knees hard. For all her verbal freedom earlier on, she couldn't think of a thing to say. And then the penny dropped.

'Oh! So this is why you were late and…'

Her eyes were becoming accustomed to the dark and she could see him nodding.

All those things she'd said! She'd behaved atrociously, hadn't even given him a chance to explain. And all because he had been a little late home. It had seemed so important at the time, but now, in contrast to Luke's news, it all seemed so petty.

'I'm sorry.'

'It wasn't your fault. Don't apologise.'

Gaby's heart squeezed inside her chest. He sounded so distant, horribly calm. This wasn't Luke! Where was the shouting and simmering? The news of Lucy's killer must have hit him hard. He must be grieving all over again.

'How are you feeling?'

He let out a short, barking laugh. 'I'll survive.'

Gaby looked at her hands. Even in the dark she couldn't look him in the eyes. 'Luke? I'm sorry about what I said too...'

'You didn't say anything that wasn't true.'

She was on her feet instantly. 'Oh, no! I was angry, but it wasn't really you I was angry with. Oh, I don't know how to explain it all...I hardly understand it myself. It's just it had been a long time coming and I finally snapped.'

Luke was standing too. 'Like I said, I'll survive.'

He went to walk past her. She grabbed his arm. 'Luke? Please!'

He turned to look at her, his face hidden as the light seeping under the lounge door made him a tall, dark silhouette. She suddenly realised she didn't have anything to say, she just didn't want them to part like this. It felt as if they were standing on opposite sides of the river with a great torrent rushing between them.

And, as if he understood, Luke leaned forward and pressed the barest of kisses on to her cheek. She shivered. His lips felt unbearably cold.

CHAPTER FOURTEEN

ODD, how an apology could sometimes thicken the ice rather than thaw it. But that was what seemed to have happened, Gaby thought, as she drove Heather home from school a few days later.

On the surface, she and Luke were all smiles and politeness, but underneath currents tugged and pulled them in different directions. Their relationship was drowning and there seemed to be nothing she could do to throw it a lifebelt.

They were both trying, to be sure. They said hello in the morning, sat and chatted in front of the TV in the evening, even kissed each other goodnight, but it all felt like an act. They might be trying, but they weren't succeeding.

Gaby didn't even feel like straightening her hair or slapping on the make-up any more, but she kept doing it anyway. To stop felt like admitting defeat.

How she longed to shove on her jeans and stuff her hair into a band any old how. But she couldn't do that, because Luke was watching. Not just the normal kind of watching, where you noticed if someone came in or left the room. Luke was watching her intently. Everything she did, everything she said. As if he were waiting for a sign. And it made her feel boxed in, trapped.

The only thing she could think of was that, when he watched her, he could see the differences between her and Lucy and it was driving a wedge even further between them. She'd stopped trying to live up to Lucy's memory; she was never going to reach the mark. It was time to stop pretending.

When they got home and Heather had run inside the house, she went to sit on the terrace. The sky was overcast and the wind bit into her face. She hunched up her shoulders and dug her fists into her pockets.

And when she could resist the idea that had been floating round her head no longer, she picked up her mobile phone and dialled the Bright Sparks Agency's number.

Luke could tell by the footsteps outside his study that it was Gaby. He looked up and waited for her knock.

'Come in.'

How formal he sounded.

She pushed the door open and he indicated she should sit in the seat in front of his desk. It was almost as if he were at work seeing a patient, so stiff was the atmosphere.

The one thing that gave him a glimmer of hope

was Gaby's clothes. She wore a faded pair of jeans, a long-sleeved top and nothing on her feet. His heart skipped a beat. Had whatever game she'd been playing ended?

'Luke, we need to talk.'

'I know.' He knew he had plenty to say to her. He'd been stupid to keep it all bottled up. He should have learned from his experience with Heather that a little openness and honesty went a long way.

'I'm leaving.'

He closed his eyes and opened them again slowly. Leaving?

'When?'

That's right. Let all the feelings come spilling out, he thought sarcastically.

She looked at the hands in her lap. 'Friday.'

He stood up. 'Friday? That's only three days from now!'

'I know.'

'But what about Heather? You can't leave us in the lurch like this!'

Yes, shouting at her was going to make her stay.

'I'm not!' Her eyes clearly showed the pain at his accusation that she would do anything to hurt Heather. 'I phoned the agency and they're sending a replacement on Monday morning. She's very good, got all the best references.'

'I don't flipping want the best references! I want you!'

She looked at him as if they both knew the sell-by date on that phrase was well and truly expired. 'No, you don't, Luke. Not really.'

'Gaby!' He skirted the desk, came to sit on the edge in front of her and gently covered her hands with his. 'That's not true. You know it's not true.'

She looked him square in the eye. 'I'm not the woman you want me to be, Luke.' Her gaze was steady.

My God, she actually believed what she was saying! How had he let things get this bad? It was his own stupid pride that had kept him from saying anything until it was too late.

'Don't say that,' he whispered, feeling a dangerous stinging at the back of his eyes. 'You are.'

She shook her head. So determined. This wasn't what he'd expected from her at all. He wasn't sure whether to be angry at her for giving up on him, or very, very scared that what she was saying was true. He looked deep into her eyes. They were filling up with tears, the sheen bringing out amber flecks he'd never seen before.

'I'm not.' A fat tear rolled down her cheek and her voice wavered. 'I've tried to be. I've tried really hard…' Her voice croaked into nothing. She opened her mouth to speak and her bottom lip wobbled so much she had to shut it again.

He pulled her up with one quick tug on her hands and hauled her into his arms. He could feel her shaking against him and he buried his face in her hair. The thought he'd never smell that delicious mixture of fresh air and daisies again was almost too much. It was just as well she couldn't see the tear that had squeezed itself out the corner of his eye against all his efforts to make it stay put.

'Stay, Gaby. Please, stay.' He peppered her hair with tiny kisses and felt, rather than heard, her sob against her chest. While she was incapable of saying the words he dreaded, he took the opportunity to do everything in his power to make her change her mind.

His hands moved up to her jaw line and he tipped her face upwards, kissing first her forehead then her eyelids, tasting the sweet saltiness of her tears. She whimpered and curled her arms around his neck, pulling him closer.

He kissed her without restraint. Now was not the time for holding back. She felt it too, he could tell. There was a quiet kind of desperation in the way they tasted each other.

She had to stay! He couldn't live without this, the sweet taste of her lips, the warm beat of her heart. He needed her more than he'd needed anything in his life before, more than food, more than air.

So what if they'd made all kinds of rules? That was before she'd announced she was deserting them. To hell with holding back! If this was the only way she'd respond to him, he'd use all the weapons in his arsenal.

He ran his hands down her torso and heard her gasp. His fingers found the hem of her top, pushed underneath it and found skin so soft he couldn't help but explore it.

Gaby's hands were no longer hooked round his neck, but undoing the top buttons of his shirt. And then things got rather hazy. All he was aware of was her hands and lips on him and vice versa. His shirt was somewhere on the floor and so was her T-shirt. The feeling of her bare skin against his chest was driving him crazy. The sensation of her teeth on his earlobe almost sent him completely over the edge.

He reached for the hooks on the back of her bra and breathed a silent thank you that her choice in underwear was as uncomplicated as the rest of her wardrobe. He slid one strap off and kissed the flesh of her shoulder. She stiffened against him.

'What?' he murmured, the fingers of the other hand sliding under the other strap and sending it the way of the first.

'Luke, stop.'

He kissed a trail from her shoulder to her ear, then paused. 'Seriously?'

'Yes.' Her voice was shaky, but that horrible determination was back.

'Why?'

She folded her arms across herself and stepped back. 'You can't really think this is a good idea?'

He looked at her. Didn't know what to say. It had been the best idea he'd had at the time. Did that count?

She frowned and shook her head. 'You're not going to make me stay this way, Luke. It would only make things worse.'

It would? From where he was standing things had been going a whole lot better than they had been for the last few weeks.

Her voice was a whisper as she bent to pick her top up from the floor. 'You know it's a bad idea. It doesn't change anything between us. It would only make things more painful in the long run, for us and for Heather. It's better to make a clean break now before anyone gets too attached, too involved.

I already am too involved, he wanted to scream. I love you! You can't get much more involved than that.

Instead he turned away slightly while she pulled her top over her head.

'You can't make me stay this way, you know. It's not playing fair.'

'I wasn't—'

'Yes, you were. You were manipulating the situation, capitalising on a weakness.'

'I thought all was fair in love and war.' That was a stupid thing to say. But he was embarrassed because she was right—he had been playing dirty.

He looked at his shirt on the floor, but refused to pick it up. He was going to make this as hard on her as possible. He decided on another tack.

'What about Heather? She's going to be devastated if you leave.'

He saw pain and irritation flash in her eyes. Good. Keep her off balance.

'I know she's going to be upset, but she'll get through it. You've got each other now. It's better I go before she guesses there was anything more between us.' She gave him a hard look. 'You're still not playing clean, Luke.'

'What do you expect?'

She sighed, looking suddenly very weary. 'Nothing else, I suppose.' She shrugged. 'But I don't appreciate it. My decision is final. You're just going to have to respect it and stop trying to manipulate me.'

Like hell he was!

The sound of the zip as she did up her case seemed very loud in the otherwise silent house. Gaby looked around the room. Her bags lay in a neat row on the bed. All the clutter, the evidence of her life here, was gone. And in a few hours she'd be gone too.

Jules had offered her the use of her spare room again and, since she didn't think the entente cordiale between her and her mother would stand the strain of living together, she was going to be right back where she'd started before she met Luke and Heather.

She closed her eyes and willed them to stay dry as she thought about leaving them behind. It didn't matter to her heart that Luke didn't love her back— it didn't care. It just wanted him more than ever. It was clearly insane.

And Luke hadn't helped matters over the last few days either. He'd tried every kind of tactic to make her stay: guilt, pity, emotional blackmail about Heather, feigned helplessness with the kitchen appliances. The man didn't know when to stop.

But maybe it was better this way. If he'd been understanding, she'd always have wondered if she'd made the right decision. The fact he was trying every way he knew to bend her will to his just proved to her she was right about him.

Don't let any man shape you...

She shrugged on her jacket and found her car keys. The last school run.

Heather was one of the last ones out of the school gates. She was dragging her backpack behind her so it scraped along the path. She got into the passenger seat, did up her seat belt and sat hugging her bag.

'You're not really going today, are you, Gaby?'

Gaby took her hand off her keys and left them sitting in the ignition. She looked across at Heather, the forlorn expression on the girl's face making her feel heartsick.

'Yes, I am, Heather.' No point in sugaring the pill. 'I promise I'll call and write. We can be penfriends.'

'Dad said you might not go.'

Did he now?

'I'm sorry, sweetie, but your Dad's wrong. It's time I went back to London. Teresa is a lovely lady. You'll really like her.'

'I don't want Teresa.'

Gaby exhaled and eased the building tension in her neck by rolling her head from side to side. Heather couldn't know she had her best interests at heart. She started the car and they drove home in silence.

When they got into the house, she left her keys in the hallway as usual. Heather glowered at her and stomped up to her room.

All that was left now was to wait for Luke to get home at five-thirty and she'd be on her way. She'd probably reach Jules's place around midnight, assuming she didn't get lost, that was.

She hauled her cases down the stairs and packed them into the boot of her car, all the while aware of a large, pink-rimmed pair of eyes watching her from the room across the landing.

Now that the moment was almost here her stomach was churning and her cheeks were hot. She picked up a mug for a cup of tea and it slid through her fingers, shattering on the unforgiving tiled floor. She swept up the pieces as carefully as she could through the tears streaming down her face.

Stop snivelling, woman! It was only a stupid mug.

Then she heard Luke's car in the drive and her stomach rolled so violently that she actually thought she was going to be sick. She scrubbed her eyes with the heels of her hands to remove any traces of moisture and stood up straight.

As she entered the entrance hall, she saw Heather flying down the stairs towards her, a wild look on her face. When she reached the bottom she threw herself at Gaby and clung to her. Gaby squeezed her eyes shut and hugged back. She'd lost her heart to Heather in a completely different way from the other children she'd grown attached to.

The fact that she'd been thinking of marrying her father made her feel more like a daughter, and leaving her was one of the most painful things she'd ever had to do. She kissed the top of Heather's head and prayed silently that one day she'd understand.

Luke found them in the hallway like that. He opened the door and forgot to move any further, all the cold air rushing in past him as a lump grew in his throat.

'I thought you were going to be my new mummy,' Heather mumbled between sniffs.

The look of shock on Gaby's face cut him like a knife.

'Oh, no, sweetie! I'm not... It isn't like that...I'm just the nanny.'

Just the nanny. He thought of the diamond ring hidden in his sock drawer and felt such a fool. She looked at him for help.

He wanted to leave her to it, to punish her for throwing his unspoken promise of happiness back in his face, but it was more important to soothe Heather than it was to get even with Gaby.

His voice was hoarse when he spoke. 'Gaby's right, darling. She could never replace your mummy.'

Hard words, but they were the truth. However much he'd wanted the dream to come real, it had never been truly within his grasp. Gaby's face was a picture of hurt. What did she want, for goodness' sake? She was the one walking away. It was her decision to take their future and dump it in the dustbin, not his.

Heather wrenched herself away from Gaby and turned to face him. He knew that look. Laser vision.

'You should make her stay, Dad!'

I tried. You don't know how hard I tried.

'You've ruined everything, just like you always do!'

And then she turned and ran up the stairs, sobbing all the way. Luke looked at Gaby. She looked so miserable that he forgot all his anger and just wanted to go to her and gather her in his arms. He couldn't believe she was really doing this. All week he'd kidded himself he'd find a way to make her stay.

She picked up her handbag and walked towards him. He stood aside to let her pass and watched her as she walked down the path towards her waiting car. Then his eyes fell on something shiny on the console table. Her keys. Before he had time to analyse what he was doing, his fingers closed over them and dropped them into his pocket.

Sure enough, she was back a few seconds later. Her gaze flicked to the table.

'Where are they, Luke?'

'I—'

'Give them to me!' She looked as if she were at breaking point. He thought of Heather and how prolonging this would only make it harder for her. His hand, still inside his pocket, felt the cold metal of her keys.

He'd failed.

Nothing he could do, nothing he could say, could make her love him enough. Time to face facts and stop fooling himself.

He hooked the keyring with his index finger and pulled it out of his pocket and dropped it in her waiting palm.

'Goodbye, Luke.'

He nodded. It was the only thing he could do. His mouth just wouldn't frame a farewell—refused.

She walked to her car and, moments later, he heard the rumble of the engine. It was only as the car was slowly accelerating down the lane that he started to run.

'Don't go!' he yelled, his breath coming in drags.

But she didn't stop. If anything she went faster.

This couldn't really be happening. He had to stop her, make her see sense.

His legs pounded as he sprinted up the lane after her. He ran until there was no way he'd catch her up, and then he ran some more. And finally, as he watched her car turn from the lane on to the hill that led out of the village, he stopped and used the last bit of oxygen available to him in one more shout.

'I love you!'

After a near miss on the hill, Gaby pulled to a stop and let the tears out. She'd been so tempted to slam the brakes on and go running back to Luke when she'd seen him following her in her rear-view mirror.

It had taken every last bit of her willpower to push her foot down harder on the accelerator, but she'd made her decision and she was sticking to it. She'd shrivel up and die if she had to endure another relationship like her marriage.

When she thought she was safe to drive again, she put the car in gear and headed for the main road that would take her back to London. She couldn't handle the motorway in her present mood. Thankfully, the traffic wasn't too heavy for a Friday night and she made good time.

Just outside Exeter she heard her mobile ring. It was Luke. The special ring tone on her phone only confirmed what her instincts told her. She ignored it.

Five minutes later it rang again. And five minutes after that. If she hadn't been doing seventy miles an hour she'd have switched it off. When it rang for the seventh time she lost her rag and swore at the dimly lit road in front of her.

That was it. Driving with a phone like a time bomb in the passenger seat, always waiting for it to go off, was dangerous. She pulled into the next truck stop and grabbed her phone, meaning to stab the off button, but something made her call him back. He'd just keep ringing if she didn't lay down the law.

'Luke?' She made sure her voice was brisk and businesslike.

His was anything but. 'Gaby? Thank God! I've been trying to get hold of you for ages. It's—'

'It's got to stop, Luke.'

'You don't understand.' She was about to say she

understood perfectly when he added, 'It's Heather. She's run away. The police are on their way and they told me to think of anywhere she might go and I've tried everywhere, Gaby. I just can't think of anywhere else. Please? Can you think of anything?'

The panic in his voice sent her heart racing. Whatever their problems, she wasn't going to sit idly by while Heather was missing.

'Have you tried the Allfords? Her other friends?'

'Everyone I can think of. I've been into the village to see if she'd gone on to the pontoons or the swing park, but there's no sign of her. Nobody's seen her either.'

'I can't think of anything else, honestly I can't. Don't worry, Luke. We'll find her. Just stay put in case she turns up—'

'That's what the police said to do, but I feel so useless!'

'It's going to be okay.'

'I can't lose her, Gaby!' His voice was breaking. 'Not after everything else.'

No, not after losing his wife too. She nodded—stupid because he couldn't see her—but the lump in her throat was stopping the words from coming out.

'Sit tight. I'm coming home.'

It seemed as if every light was on in the Old Boathouse when she pulled up outside it. She jumped out the car, ignoring the protests of her stiff legs, and ran up the path. The door was ajar.

'Luke? Heather?'

No answer.

Where was he? He should be here! Unless… unless the police had called because they'd found her somewhere. Her blood ran cold as the possible outcomes played in her mind.

And then she went very still.

He wouldn't, would he?

What if this was a stunt to get her back here? This was some kind of sick joke if it was. She shook her head. Luke would never do that to her.

'Luke?'

Where the hell was he? She didn't want to believe the doubts trying to creep into her brain.

She looked in his study, the lounge, the kitchen. Nothing. She was just about to go and check upstairs when a movement out of the window caught her eye.

He was outside on the jetty. It was only then that she noticed the open door and the draught rushing into the room. In a few moments she was through the door and jumping down the steps.

'Luke!'

He turned and she felt so ashamed for doubting him that she almost turned tail and ran the other way. No one could doubt he'd been telling the truth if they'd seen the haunted look on his face. She should have known, believed in him a little more. He might be the most stubborn man she had ever known, too pig-headed to know when to stop sometimes, but he wasn't one to deceive.

'What is it? Luke?'

The lost expression on his face was beginning to worry her.

'The dinghy…'

She looked at the dinghy, or at least where the dinghy was supposed to be. All she saw was black water slapping against the jetty.

CHAPTER FIFTEEN

HALF the village GOT into their boats of varying shapes and sizes to help search for Heather. It wasn't going to be an easy task, even with the clear sky and the bright moon to aid them. They started searching the immediate area first. Hopefully, there would be no need to widen the search later.

Just upstream of the village the river widened. It was a popular place for locals and weekend sailors alike to moor their boats. A small inflatable dinghy could easily be hidden amongst the bobbing yachts and cruisers.

Luke held his torch and directed its beam at the stony beach to his right. Ben had offered to take him and Gaby out to search in the ferryboat. That daft police officer had tried to convince him to stay at the house. No way! How could he sit at home while his daughter was lost on the river?

'Heather!' His voice was getting hoarse.

Identical shouts from other parts of the river echoed back to him across the water at random intervals. The torch beam wobbled and refused to shine where he wanted it to. He willed his aching arm to stay still and steadied it with the other hand. His eyes were getting tired and every large rock was starting to look like a capsized boat.

'Luke? Why don't you sit down for a second, take a rest?' Gaby's hand rested on his shoulder, but he shrugged it away.

'I can't.'

'You need to.'

Didn't she understand? 'It's been five hours since she disappeared! How can I rest? Tell me that!'

She took the torch gently from his hands. 'I'll take over, just for a few minutes. Luke, please? You're no good if you're too tired to see straight.' She was right. But then he was as good as useless anyway. Useless as a father, useless as a husband-and two women had confirmed it, so there wasn't any doubt about that one.

Why? Why had he let Heather believe Gaby might stay? It had been stupid. Probably because he hadn't wanted to believe it himself, but he should have been honest, with himself and with Heather. Then she might be tucked up in bed rather than out risking hypothermia, or worse.

He closed his eyes and immediately opened them again. The images of *or worse* couldn't be allowed to play behind his eyelids.

'I can see something!'

Gaby's shriek had him into the stern where she was standing in seconds. 'Over there! Near that big boat!'

Ben brought the ferry closer.

Sure enough, bumping against the side of some weekend cruiser, was a small grey dinghy.

'Give me that!' He snatched the torch out of Gaby's hands, but she didn't react, she just leaned over the edge of the boat next to him, straining to see. And then her hands flew to her mouth and she gasped.

The dinghy was empty.

'No!' The word came from his mouth without any conscious decision on his part.

If Heather was in this water, even though she was a fairly strong swimmer for her age, she wouldn't stand much of a chance. It was cold. The currents were swift. In the dark it would be easy to get disoriented.

He put his head in his hands and let out a few ragged breaths. His lungs seemed to be squeezing, depriving him of air.

Gaby's arms came round him and he buried his head in her hair. 'I don't know what to do.'

Gaby held him tight. 'It doesn't mean anything, Luke. It could have come loose on its own. She might not even have been in the boat in the first place.'

He wished he could believe her. She sounded so sure.

'Look at me.'

He lifted his head and saw the fierce determination in her eyes. This was why he loved her—her strength, her compassion. For a while he'd thought it had been a mirage, but he'd been right about her all along.

'We're not giving up,' she warned him. 'Heather's always in a rush. Maybe she didn't tie it up properly, or even...' her eyes glazed over '...forgot.'

'What? What are you thinking?'

'It might be nothing...but...'

He almost shook her. 'Gaby!'

She jumped. 'I just remembered that day we went out for a picnic and how the boat almost floated away...'

A small flicker of hope ignited inside him. 'You think she got out of the boat and forgot to tie it up?'

'More than that! Think, Luke! She loved that place where she built her camp. Maybe she went back there!'

Good grief, she could be right.

'Ben!' he shouted, feeling the blood coursing in his ears. 'Upstream, as quick as you can! I'll show you exactly where when we get near.'

They clung to each other as Ben steered the ferryboat to the spot where they'd had their picnic. They weren't quite close enough yet. What was taking so long? He shone the torch on the water between boat and beach. He could make it. He jumped out of the boat and floundered a second before he found his feet.

Gaby watched him wading through the water, her heart cramping with each beat. She grabbed the torch Luke had dropped and took a long look at the water below. Then she hoisted her legs over the side and followed him.

The shock of the icy cold forced a cry from her lips, but she pushed her legs hard through the water until she caught up with Luke on the beach, who was staring blindly into the shadows.

'Here.' She thrust the torch at him and he took off with it. Gaby did her best to keep up, but he was darting this way and that and she often found herself walking into an invisible branch as the torch beam danced away.

'I can't find it!' he yelled back at her. 'It all looks so different in the dark.'

He turned away again and her surroundings melted into the darkness.

'Luke, I can't—'

Her shin made contact with something extremely hard and she stumbled. Her arms flew forwards instinctively and skin ripped from her palms as they bore the brunt of the impact. She refused to cry out. It didn't matter. Finding Heather mattered.

'Gaby?'

'Over here. I tripped over a blasted rock.'

The torch beam bobbed as he came closer. She tried to wave him on as she picked herself up and tried to brush the grit from her raw skin.

'Luke!'

'Are you hurt?' He caught up with her, breathless.

'Yes. No. Never mind. Look! This is it! The place we built the camp fire.'

He swung the torch downwards. 'You're sure?'

'Yes! This is the rock we sat on. That knobbly bit

kept sticking into my bottom. It was really uncomfortable.'

He ran his hand along the lichen-covered surface. 'You're right! That means…'

Gaby was way ahead of him. She lunged off to the right in the direction of the bush that Heather had claimed as her hidey-hole. Then she froze. They both did.

A twig had snapped somewhere in front of them.

It could be anything. A rabbit or a fox. She looked over her shoulder at Luke. And then there was another sound. A distinctly human-sounding sniff.

'Heather?'

Luke quickly illuminated the spot she was pointing to and she dived forward and ripped the makeshift 'door' off the opening. Even though she was blocking the light, she could make out a familiar form curled into a ball, a large pair of eyes watching her.

Gaby started to cry as she jammed her shoulders between a couple of branches.

'Oh, sweetheart! We've been looking all over for you.'

'Heather!' Luke almost screamed somewhere behind her.

Heather didn't move a muscle. She didn't even blink. Gaby was about to say something soothing when Luke's elbow knocked her in the head. There was no way he was going to fit! It was only just big enough for one small girl and the top half of one small woman.

'Luke! There's no room! You're going to have to let me back out first!'

Luke muttered something under his breath, but she felt him step away. She looked back at Heather. The poor girl was shaking like a leaf, even though she had her thick coat on.

'Come on, Heather.' She held out her hand. Heather shook her head.

Okay. Not just cold, scared too.

'It's okay.' She held out her hand.

'What the heck is taking so long?' Luke's voice boomed through the silence.

Gaby twisted as far as the bush would allow her to. The light of the torch in her eyes almost blinded her. She pushed it upwards so she could see his face. 'Just give us a second, will you?'

Luke looked as if he wanted to uproot the bush with his bare hands, but he nodded, his mouth a thin line.

She turned back to Heather.

'Come on. No one's cross. We're just so relieved to have found you.'

'Really?'

Gaby nodded. Heather's icy little fingers made contact with hers. Slowly they edged their way out of the camp together. Heather stayed close behind her, using her as a shield.

'Don't shout at me, Daddy!' Her voice was thick with tears. 'I didn't mean to! But the dinghy floated away and I was stuck…and…and I didn't know how to get back.'

Gaby stepped aside and let Luke scoop Heather up into his arms. He hugged her so hard she thought her ribs would crack. Gaby pressed her fingers to her mouth and said a silent thank you as her eyes filled up. She loved this man and this little girl so much. Even if she wasn't going to be a permanent fixture in their lives, she would have been devastated if anything had happened to either of them.

Ten minutes later they were back in Ben's boat heading for home. He'd radioed ahead with the good news and an ambulance was going to be waiting for them at Lower Hadwell to check Heather over. Luke seemed pretty sure there was nothing to worry about, but she guessed nobody was taking any chances.

She stood up in the cabin with Ben while Luke and Heather sat further down the boat, huddled together under an old blanket. Gaby bit her lip and held on to the side of the boat tightly. She wanted so much to join them, but it was a private moment between father and daughter and she had resigned, remember. From being the nanny and being part of their family.

'Why did you run away, Heather? Where were you going?' Luke asked gently. Gaby tried not to listen, but it was very hard in a boat this size.

Heather looked down into her lap. 'I thought you and Gaby were going to get married.'

'What gave you that idea?'

She looked up at him, unimpressed. 'I'm not a kid, you know. You were both giving each other those looks Gaby says I give Liam.'

Gaby didn't know whether to laugh or cry.

'I thought we were going to be a proper family.' Heather's voice almost faded away entirely. 'I really wanted Gaby to be my mum. You should have made her stay, Dad.'

Luke hugged his daughter to him and placed a kiss on top of her head. Then he looked at Gaby. She quickly stared into the distance and tried to make out she wasn't listening.

'Heather,' he began. 'You know when you first came to live with me and all I did was tell you what to do all the time?'

'Yeah, it was a real drag.'

Gaby squashed a smile.

'You didn't like it much when I made you do things you didn't want to do, did you?'

'No.'

'Well, it's kind of the same. Gaby wants to go and I can't change that even if I want to, Heather.'

And he'd certainly tried every sneaky trick in the book to stop her. Why was that, anyway? She'd been so busy reacting to the fact she felt pushed around that she hadn't asked herself that question. If Lucy had been the be-all and end-all, and Gaby was a pale imitation, why did he want her to stay?

Perhaps, he thought she was close enough to second best. Once upon a time she'd have settled for that, but now she needed more. She needed to be wanted for who she was, not for what she could be if someone pushed hard enough.

'You could have tried harder,' Heather piped up.

'No, Heather. It doesn't work like that. If Gaby needs to go and get another job somewhere else, then we need to let her. It's not up to us. It's her choice.'

Gaby frowned. Big words from the man who'd hidden her keys earlier on. She turned away and looked up at the sky. It was one of those magical starry nights. Thank goodness the magic had worked and Heather was safe.

'Pretty, isn't it?'

She'd almost forgotten Ben was standing next to her, he'd been so quiet.

'Yes, it is. I wonder how they get so pretty.'

Ben snorted and she was suddenly reminded of their first meeting.

'They don't *do* anything, do they?' he said, slowing the engine as they neared the pontoons at Lower Hadwell. 'They don't try to be beautiful. They just are what they are.'

Gaby woke early the next morning, despite the late hour she'd crawled into bed. She focused on the cream walls of the Old Boathouse guest room. She could almost imagine that the past twenty-four hours had been a dream and that she was going to walk into the kitchen and start making breakfast as usual. But last night had been anything but usual.

Thank goodness the paramedics had declared

Heather shaken but otherwise fine and had been happy to let her go home with a doctor in residence.

Gaby threw the duvet back and stood up. The plan had been to sling on what she'd worn yesterday. She went over to the radiator where she'd hung her jeans. Wet and muddy. Yuck.

She threw her fleece over her head, stuffed her feet in her shoes and decided to run out to the car and pull something clean from her case. She crept out on to the landing, only to meet Luke emerging from his room, fully dressed.

'Like the outfit,' he said, looking her up and down.

She blushed and hoped the fleece was long enough to hide her knickers. The clear look of male appreciation on Luke's face only increased her fear that it was a couple of inches shy.

'I'm going to the car…to get something dry.'

Luke just smiled and her silly heart went all giggly and batted its eyelashes.

'I wanted to thank you, Gaby—for coming back to help. We might not have found her if it weren't for you.'

He took hold of her hands and goosebumps broke out on her bare legs.

Oh, you bad girl! You want him to kiss you.

And, even as she told herself what a daft idea it was, they seemed to lean closer together. She closed her eyes and waited for the soft touch of his lips upon hers.

It never came.

She opened her eyes again. He was looking at her

as if he wanted to kiss her and, just as she thought he was going to follow through, he let go of her hands and backed away.

'Thanks,' he said again simply.

'It was nothing. I couldn't stand by when Heather was in trouble, could I? What would you have done if you'd lost your daughter as well as your wife?' She was babbling. 'I mean, you were devastated when Lucy died. How would you have coped without the one thing you had left of her?'

Luke tipped his head to one side and lines appeared on his forehead. 'I was sad when Lucy died, yes. Devastated for Heather. No one should have to go through that. But I'd already lost her. Our marriage was on the rocks, Gaby.'

'How awful!'

'Not really. Once I got over the shock, it was actually quite a relief.'

She blinked.

'We should never have got married in the first place. I can't regret it entirely, though. I got a wonderful daughter out of it.'

Lucy? Not perfect? Things weren't making sense.

'But I thought…I'd better get my things from the car.' She scurried down the stairs, refusing to look at him. Once she was fully dressed she'd feel less disoriented.

After breakfast Gaby took a walk on the beach to try and get things straight in her head. It seemed that

Luke and Lucy's marriage hadn't been the grand passion she'd imagined it to be. So why had she spent the last few weeks killing herself trying to fill Lucy's shoes? Now she looked at her behaviour it seemed to make no sense. Only that she'd felt she wasn't good enough for Luke.

It had been that same cold feeling in the pit of her stomach that she'd had throughout her marriage. She was so scared of losing Luke she'd have done anything to keep him. Including shaping herself into the image of his perfect woman. Only it had turned out that the image she'd used as her template hadn't been so perfect after all.

All those years she'd made herself into what David had wanted her to be and it had been a disaster. It had only pushed him further away and killed her spirit.

She came to a halt and sat on a large branch that had fallen from one of the trees overhanging the water line. The bark was gone and the wood underneath had been washed smooth by the tide.

All this time she had been trying to avoid making the same mess of her relationship with Luke that she'd made of her marriage. Only she hadn't avoided her mistakes, she'd repeated them.

All that stuff she'd recited to herself about needing to be free to make her own decisions had been stuffed in the cupboard gathering cobwebs as soon as love had come into the equation. She'd set about transforming herself without even bothering to find out what Luke really wanted.

And if his behaviour during the last few days was anything to go by, he wanted her, the unvarnished Gaby. Messy hair and all. She gasped and covered her mouth with her hand.

Oh, you stupid, stupid woman! All that time you spent trying to draw him to you, you were pushing him away.

How had she missed it? She almost wanted to laugh, it was so ridiculous.

A warm glow of hope began to tickle her tummy. Perhaps it wasn't too late. Perhaps they could have a happy ending after all. It all depended on what Luke wanted. One problem though: she was too terrified to ask.

Luke watched Gaby walk back up the beach and up to the kitchen door. He felt sick. What if he never saw her again? He wanted to run to her, pull her into his arms and convince her to stay using all the dirty tricks he could think of.

Only he didn't. He started clearing the breakfast dishes.

He had to respect her decision. Just like he'd learned how to give Heather her freedom, he had to give Gaby hers. He'd already squeezed one woman so hard in an effort to hang on to her that she'd popped out of his grasp and into the arms of another.

He felt the diamond ring in the back pocket of his jeans. He'd found the box while he'd been hunting for matching socks this morning and he'd taken the ring out and put it in his pocket. A good luck charm. It would always be waiting for her, whenever she wanted to claim it.

Gaby entered the kitchen and he pulled his hand out of his pocket. She looked as if she were trying to work out what he was thinking and he quickly relaxed his face into a neutral expression.

'Well, this is it, then. Time to go.'

'Yes.' Good. Keep it plain and simple, non-committal.

She scuffed the floor with the tip of her trainer. 'I could stay a bit longer, you know.' She glanced up at him through her lashes, then went back to examining her shoe. 'If you and Heather need a familiar face, after the shock you've both had…'

'Heather and I will manage, Gaby. And Teresa will be here on Monday. You just do what you've got to do.'

A wave of irritation passed over her features. 'All right, then. I'll just get my coat.'

He followed her out into the hallway, where she took an inordinately long time stuffing her arms into the sleeves of her jacket and doing up every last button. Then she walked across to him and stood directly in front of him, her eyes large and searching.

'Goodbye, Luke.'

'Goodbye, Gaby.'

She stood on tiptoe and placed a feather-light kiss on his lips. Good grief, she wasn't making this easy! Just as she was pulling back, she seemed to have second thoughts and went in for another kiss, deeper, sweeter.

This was torture! He loved this woman—so much the words were ringing round his head and it was all he could do not to shout them out. But he couldn't say it. It would just put pressure on her.

Instead he put every ounce of the feeling into his kiss, but even then he let her take the lead. He wasn't going to make the same mistake as last time. When her hands came up round his neck, he jammed his own into his pockets. And when she finally broke it off, he did nothing to stop her.

She looked so sad. As if he'd done something wrong. His neutral mask slipped as he saw the pain in her eyes. He tried to give a little smile, but he suspected it was more of a grimace and gave up.

'I'll go and say goodbye to Heather.'

'I'll just go and check you've left nothing in the mud room,' he said, in a desperate effort to break the spell before he caved in completely. Distance. He needed distance. He spent as long as he could rearranging the wellington boots.

Just as he re-entered the hall, empty handed, he heard a jangle of metal. Gaby jumped away from the hall table. Her keys were lying on the table. They hadn't been there a few minutes ago.

'Anything?' she asked.

'Nope. All gone.'

She fidgeted. 'Actually, I think I have one of your umbrellas in my car. I'll just go and fetch it.' Her gaze skittered briefly to the keys and then she was out of the door.

Luke felt so stupidly happy, he wanted to dance and shout and sing. She *wanted* him to steal her keys again! His heart began to pound.

He tried to compose his face as saw her coming up the garden path. It took all his willpower to keep his hand from reaching out and closing over her keyring.

No, if Gaby wanted to stay, she was going to have to do it on her own, not because he'd left her no other choice.

She walked brightly in and handed him a golfing umbrella. 'There.'

'Thanks.' He took it from her and leaned it up against the wall.

Her eyes flicked to the keys still on the table and, while her mouth maintained a smile, it died in her eyes.

They walked down the path together and he stood outside the front gate and watched her get into her car She didn't even look at him. When she started the car and pulled away, all the hope that had been building inside him crumbled like a dried out sandcastle.

Gaby looked in her rear-view mirror as she drove away slowly. Any second now he'd start running. She picked up speed. Had he grown roots or something? Why wasn't he moving?

Don't you dare cry! This is what you wanted, remember? To make your own decisions. You decided it was better to go, so go. Luke is respect-ing your decision, just like you asked him to. Nothing to cry about there.

Only suddenly she wasn't respecting her own choice any more. Why was she driving away with her heart breaking when she really wanted to stay?

She eased off the accelerator slightly. In her mirror she could still see Luke standing at the bottom of the lane. The same ache was etched all over his face too.

The car skidded to a stop as clarity hit her like a slap round the head.

She'd been so fixated on being free to make her own choices that she hadn't even stopped to consider whether her choice had been the right one.

She swung the door open and left it gaping and started to run. The car engine was still purring behind her, keys swinging in the ignition, but she didn't care. Her legs were pumping as fast as they could as she raced back towards him. One shoe flew off. She left it where it landed.

He threw back his head and laughed with joy, but he didn't move and she didn't want him to. This was one journey she had to make all on her own.

She was almost there, despite the fact that laughing and running and crying all at the same time was not a good combination if she wanted to travel in a straight line.

How could she have doubted his love? It was written all over his face, plain to see.

She covered the last foot or two by launching herself into his arms and wrapping her legs around his middle. And then he was kissing her face and she his and they were squeezing each other so tight she was sure they'd end up a little unconscious heap in the mud.

'I love you, Gaby Michaels.'

She grinned up at him as he lowered her to the ground. 'I know. I love you too. Can I stay? Please?'

He laughed. 'I thought you'd never ask! Only… you're not going to start wearing those scary shoes again, are you?'

I won't if you don't want me to, she almost blurted.

'Actually, they hurt like hell and I live in fear of spraining my ankle, so I think they'll only get occasional use.'

He kissed her again, then broke off to whisper in her ear. 'Actually, there is something I insist you do if you stay.'

She frowned. 'Luke Armstrong! You were doing so well. Don't spoil it now.'

He pulled something shiny from his pocket. 'You've got to wear this.' He held a diamond ring up to her hand, but stopped before it circled her finger. 'But only if you want to.'

She kissed him in such a way he couldn't doubt her answer. 'Of course I want to, you grumpy old man!'

He started to slide the ring on to her finger, but almost dropped it as they were distracted by a scream from an upstairs window. They had an audience. Heather was clapping and jumping up and down.

They smiled at each other. 'Put it on properly, then,' he said, nodding to the ring dangling from her knuckle.

'You don't know when to stop, do you?'

She eased the ring the rest of the way.

He kissed her hand and looked deep into her eyes. Then he kissed her mouth, his lips warm and firm and full of certainty.

'Nope. You're right,' he whispered into her ear. 'I have no idea how to stop loving you.'

FREE!

2 Books
and a surprise gift!

We would like to take this opportunity to thank you for reading this Mills & Boon® book by offering you the chance to take FOUR more specially selected titles from the Romance series absolutely FREE! We're also making this offer to introduce you to the benefits of the Mills & Boon® Reader Service™—

- ★ FREE home delivery
- ★ FREE gifts and competitions
- ★ FREE monthly Newsletter
- ★ Exclusive Reader Service offers
- ★ Books available before they're in the shops

Accepting these FREE books and gift places you under no obligation to buy, you may cancel at any time, even after receiving your free shipment. Simply complete your details below and return the entire page to the address below. You don't even need a stamp!

YES! Please send me 4 free Romance books and a surprise gift. I understand that unless you hear from me, I will receive 6 superb new titles every month for just £2.89 each, postage and packing free. I am under no obligation to purchase any books and may cancel my subscription at any time. The free books and gift will be mine to keep in any case.

N7ZEF

Ms/Mrs/Miss/Mr ....Initials..................................

BLOCK CAPITALS PLEASE

Surname ....

Address..

....

....Postcode ....

Send this whole page to:
UK: FREEPOST CN8I, Croydon, CR9 3WZ